Also by Susan Gabriel

Fiction

Lily's Song
(sequel to *The Secret Sense of Wildflower*)

Temple Secrets

Trueluck Summer

Grace, Grits and Ghosts: Southern Short Stories

Seeking Sara Summers

Circle of the Ancestors

Quentin and the Cave Boy

Nonfiction

Fearless Writing for Women:
Extreme Encouragement and Writing Inspiration

Available at all booksellers
in print, ebook and audio formats.

The Secret Sense of Wildflower

Susan Gabriel

Wild Lily Arts

The Secret Sense of Wildflower
Copyright © 2012 by Susan Gabriel

Library of Congress Control Number: 2012936549

ISBN: 978-0-9835882-3-8

Wild Lily Arts

Printed in the United States of America.

For my daughters
Krista and Stacey

Consider the lilies of the field, how they grow:
they neither toil nor spin;
and yet I say to you that even Solomon in all his glory
was not arrayed like one of these.

Matthew 6:28-29

CHAPTER ONE

There are two things I am afraid of. One is dying young. The other is Johnny Monroe. Whenever I see him I get a creepy feeling that crawls up the length of my spine. Daddy used to say that fear is a friend that teaches us life isn't to be played with. Friends like this I can live without.

On my way to the graveyard I run into Johnny standing by the road. His smile shows shreds of chewing tobacco caked around the edges of his teeth. But the scariest thing is the look in his eyes when he sees me or my sisters. He is like a wildcat stalking his next meal. People living in the mountains know that anytime you come across a wildcat you don't look it in the eye or make sudden moves. Every time I see Johnny Monroe I slow down and stare at the tops of my shoes.

"Hey, Louisa May." Johnny drawls out my name. At sixteen, he is nearly four years older than me, and is a good six inches taller, even slouched. He dropped out of school in the sixth grade and spends a lot of time just standing around.

I wish I'd turned back when it first occurred to me. Aunt Sadie, Daddy's sister, calls this my secret sense. The secret sense is a nudge from somewhere deep inside that keeps you out of harm's way if you listen to it. Aunt Sadie is full of ideas that most people don't cater to. Not to mention that she never married, a fact that makes some people nervous, and sometimes wears a fedora. Sadie collects herbs and roots to make mountain remedies. People come from all over to have her doctor them with red clover blossoms and honey to cure their whooping cough or to get catnip mint to soothe their colicky babies. She also makes the best blackberry wine in three counties.

"What's the matter, girl, you deaf?" Johnny says.

"I'm not talking to you," I hiss behind clinched teeth.

"But you're talking to me right now," he says. He grins.

"Go away," I say. I focus on the worn spot at the end of my shoe and roll my shoulders forward so Johnny will stop staring at my chest, even though there's nothing much to stare at.

"Where's that sister of yours?" Johnny asks.

I know he means Meg. Johnny asks after her every chance he gets.

"I wouldn't mind getting her out behind those bushes. She's not scrawny like you are, Louisa May." Johnny laughs.

An empty tin can sits on the ground next to him and he spits a mouthful of tobacco juice toward the can. It pings against the side. Only Johnny would make a sport of spitting into a can with "cling peaches" written on the side. He could just as well spit on the road, but he appears to take pride in the "ping," like a dart thrower hitting the bright red bull's-eye in the center of the board.

"Maybe I should just settle for scrawny," he says. But it seems he's talking more to himself than to me.

To keep the words from spewing out, I bite my bottom lip hard. I want to call Johnny a low-life and a good-for-nothing, which is exactly what he is. Instead, I shuffle forward and don't look up again until I reach the bend in the road. When I glance back Johnny is still watching me and licks his lips.

Before Johnny, I can't say I ever hated anyone. I've come close a couple of times, with Doc Lester and Preacher Evans, who have the obnoxious habit of acting like they are better than everybody else. They remind me of gnats and I just want to take a newspaper and shoo them away. But Johnny is more like a black widow spider. He stands on that corner every day hoping some unsuspecting girl will fall into his web.

In my weaker moments, I feel sorry for Johnny. Life must be desperate and lonely standing on that road, kicking rocks all day. Not to mention that he doesn't have a mother. Word is she died from tuberculosis when he was nine. Mama said once that his old man hates kids and would just as soon sell them if he could get a decent price.

"Hey, girl," Johnny calls after me. "Come back here and talk." But I know better than to look back.

Johnny has a sister my age named Ruby and another sister named Melody who is probably around ten by now. Ruby doesn't come to school anymore, just stays home to cook and clean for Johnny and the old man. Her younger sister Melody never even started school. I've tried to talk to Ruby a few times, but she won't have any part of people around here. Every time I see her she looks like she's made best friends with misery. She is as slight as a thirteen-year-old girl can be, but she drags herself around like she carries a fifty pound sack of potatoes on her back.

Meanwhile, Johnny stands out on that road like he's waiting for his mother to come back and make his life different than it is. That doesn't make the things he says to me right, or make Meg want to give him the time of day, but in a way I think I understand why Johnny is stuck on that road. He's waiting for a better life to show up since he's been dealt such a crummy one.

If Daddy was here he'd knock Johnny Monroe's rotten teeth right out of his head for looking at me the way Johnny does. But Daddy is one of those markers in the graveyard where if you subtract the years, you know he was thirty-eight when he died almost a year ago. Every few days I walk up the hill and sit with him and tell him about things in my life so we don't lose touch. That's where I'm headed right now. I won't tell him about Johnny, though, because I wouldn't want him to worry.

Sometimes when I'm at the graveyard I'll hear Daddy talking back to me. Mama would say that's just my imagination working overtime, but Sadie would say it's the secret sense. I'm grateful for it, whatever it is. If we run out of things to catch up on, I'll ask Daddy to talk to God for me. Mainly I have questions, like does a praying mantis really pray? And why does God send lightning to hit old dead trees? And why did Johnny Monroe have to end up here in Katy's Ridge? I've found a favorite sitting spot by Daddy's grave so I can wait for him and God to answer. They haven't so far, but I have time to wait. Time is about the only thing I have plenty of in Katy's Ridge. That, and chigger bites.

With Johnny out of sight, I quit looking at my shoes, pull back my shoulders and approach the shortcut I found to Daddy's final resting place. The old trail meanders up the mountain and to the far corner of the graveyard where they pile all the dead flowers. The path is so overgrown in spots I have to guess which way it points. And it has a footbridge built across the highest point of the stream that has only one sturdy board left. The rest I wouldn't trust to hold a cricket.

A dogwood tree on the shady side of the hill marks the beginning of the trail. That old dogwood is twisted and tangled from fighting its way toward sunlight. But all that struggling has made it beautiful. Thick underbrush hides the trail behind it like a locked gate. As far as I know, nobody else is aware of this old path. With three older sisters, who have already done everything before me, having a secret way through the woods is like finally having something of my own.

I look all around to make sure no one is watching before I enter the path. Gossip travels the grapevine in Katy's Ridge like Western Union telegrams. If anybody sees me, Mama will know in a matter of minutes. Minding your own business isn't the way of mountain people in Tennessee in 1941, though sometimes I wish it was.

The coast clear, I duck behind the tree and take the secret path. The trail travels a steep hill before it levels out and dips down into the valley again. The footbridge is about halfway between home and the graveyard.

At the bridge, I do my good luck ritual that I've used since I was a little girl. It has three parts. Daddy used to say that threes always happen in fairy tales: three wishes, three ogres, three sisters. Whenever a "three" shows up you can expect some kind of magic to take place. No matter how old I get, I'll use magic, luck, or my own prayer meeting, if it means I get safely across that bridge.

My sister, Meg, gave me a rabbit's foot key chain from Woolworth's last Christmas. I retrieve it from my pocket and squeeze out a dose of good luck. Then I ask Daddy to watch out for me, calling on God and his angels if need be. After that I kiss the dime-sized gold medallion that I have worn around my neck ever since Daddy died. The medallion used to belong to my Grandma McAllister. Engraved on it is a picture of the baby Jesus sitting on his mother's lap. I like looking at the sweet smile on her face on account of my mother hardly ever smiles anymore.

All us girls got something after Grandma McAllister died. Jo got fancy doilies and things, Amy got some of her books and Meg got a set of her dishes. I would have liked to have the books, since I've been a tomboy most of my life and was never much of a jewelry person. But Daddy said, since I got the medallion, that I was the luckiest one because Jesus' mother watches out for people. Standing at the bridge, this seems as good a time as any for her to watch out for me.

Before they moved to the United States, the McAllister's were all Catholic. Sometimes I would see Daddy cross himself the way the Catholics do. It was usually when nobody else was around. Mama's folks were Lutheran. But after Mama and Daddy moved to Katy's Ridge they joined the Baptists just to keep the peace. At least that's how Daddy put it.

Little Women is Mama's favorite book. A worn copy of it sits on her dresser right next to the King James Bible. I was named after the lady who wrote it, Louisa May Alcott. Destiny must have rewarded Mama for her devotion to the book because she gave Daddy four daughters, just like the March family in the book. My older sisters, Amy, Jo, and Meg, were each named after somebody in the book. Another sister, Beth, died two days after she was born. This explains how I ended up with the name Louisa May, because all the good names were already taken.

I am the youngest McAllister. Jo and Amy, my two older sisters, each got married last spring and live in Katy's Ridge, right down the road from our house. Meg, my closest sister in age, graduated from Rocky Bluff High School last year but still lives at home and works at the Woolworth's store in the town of Rocky Bluff. I like having Meg around because she smoothes things out between Mama and me. Even on our best days, we are like vinegar and soda, always reacting. When Meg isn't there, Mama and I do our level best to avoid each other.

The board of the old footbridge creaks and sways when I step onto it and I have to hold out my arms to steady myself. I shot up like a weed last year, from 4 feet, seven inches to 5 feet 3 and I am still not used to this willowy version of myself.

As far as I can tell, the secret to not falling is to keep your arms out and your feet moving in a straight line, which is probably the one good thing that has come from looking at my shoes so much around Johnny Monroe. While I summon my courage, I am reminded of the pictures I saw once of trapeze artists crossing a wire at a circus. My knees start to shake and I tell them to stop. If I'm not careful I could shake myself right into an early grave. I bite my lip, which for some odd reason also helps me keep my balance.

Even though I am nearly thirteen years of age, if Mama knew I was crossing this old bridge she'd give me a good talking to, using all three of my given names while she did.

Louisa May McAllister, what were you thinking? Don't you know you could fall in and bust your head against the rocks? You'd be dead in an instant. Then what would I do?

Mama has a way of asking a question that makes my head hurt.

Safe on the other side of the footbridge, I sit cross-legged on the ground and take a few deep breaths. The mountain feels solid underneath me and I thank it for holding me up. I also take time to thank Daddy, my rabbit's foot, and the mother of our good Lord, by way of Grandma McAllister, for helping me get across and not fall into the chasm.

After I begin my trek again, I follow the path that winds up the hill like a snake. At the top of the hill I push open the rusty gate at the back of the graveyard and enter. In the distance stands the willow tree draping its branches above Daddy's final resting place.

The summer before he died, we made fishing poles out of its branches and he told me stories about our people buried here, especially my baby sister Beth. He never failed to mention how old she'd be if she hadn't died, which is always one year older than me at any given moment.

It is still strange to think of Daddy being under the ground in a wooden box, even if his spirit has gone off to live in heaven. It seems like his bones would get to go, too. But Preacher says you throw off your body at the end, just like you throw off an old coat you are tired of wearing. Maybe your bones weigh you down when you get to heaven if you take them with you. I don't know.

I am one month away from my thirteenth birthday and the only girl I know who hangs out in graveyards. But if you don't mind being around dead people, it has a beautiful view overlooking the Tennessee River. Thick, old maples and oaks grace the hillside and the nearby stream empties into the river at the bottom of the hill. In the distance stands the small Baptist church practically everybody in Katy's Ridge attends. A large weeping willow grows in the center of the graveyard. A willow whose leaves sweep the ground when the wind blows, just like Mama sweeps our porch in the evenings. Last fall it wept down gold, almond-shaped leaves on top of Daddy's grave, and I knew he must be smiling because he always said he'd struck gold when I was born.

"Hi Daddy," I say to his tombstone.

I sit under the willow tree and cross my long legs up under me. With my finger, I trace the dates, 1902-1940, feeling the coldness of the stone. Daddy is the one who nicknamed me "Wildflower" when I was ten-years-old. He said the name fit me perfect since I'd sprung up here in the mountains like a wild trillium. Trillium will take your breath away if you see a patch of them. Daddy had a way with words, like a poet, and not just with me. He could make Mama smile faster than anything. Sometimes he'd get her laughing so hard she'd hold her sides till tears came to her eyes. All us kids stood around with our jaws dropped. To see Mama laugh was as rare as snow in August.

"We miss you, Daddy," I say. "All of us do, especially Mama. But we're doing all right, I guess."

He would want to know that we're doing all right and sometimes I tell him this even when we aren't.

Daddy always put his arms around Mama in the kitchen or laid an extra blanket on the bed because he knew she got cold in the middle of the night when the fire died down. No matter if he was sweating he kept Mama warm. But there aren't enough blankets in the world to make up for Daddy being gone. Sometimes I wonder if she ever gets mad at him for going away. I know I do. After the sadness gnawed me numb, I got pissed as a rattlesnake that he hadn't been more careful while working at the sawmill, and that he'd left us all alone.

"Louisa May, you fell asleep again."

The voice hovers over me and I wonder if maybe one of God's angels has come to take me to be with Daddy. Even though I am not a little girl anymore, I like thinking there are angels. When my eyes focus on what I hope will be my first celestial visitor, I see instead my sister, Jo. She is the most beautiful of all us McAllisters. She has golden blond hair the color of the inside of a honey comb, unlike my tangled dirty mop of curls, as Mama likes to call them. Like honey, Jo is also very sweet, but she isn't the angel I hoped for.

"My name is Wildflower," I say half asleep, rolling over on Daddy's grave.

When I was little, Daddy and I used to take naps together on Saturday afternoons like this one. He'd be folded up on one end of the sofa and I'd be on the other, our toes touching, until Mama made us get up to do our chores.

"Mama has dinner ready," Jo says. She taps the bottom of my shoes with hers.

"How's Daniel?" I ask, opening one eye. Her husband is almost as sweet as she is.

"He's fine, and he's waiting on his dinner, too." She reaches down to pull me up.

I brush away the pieces of leaves and dirt that leave spider web patterns on my legs. Jo and I are the same height now, but I haven't filled out like her yet.

"Mama worries about you coming up here all the time," Jo says. "I don't see why you bother. It takes forever to get here."

I don't tell Jo about my secret shortcut. If she knew about the old footbridge she'd probably make me promise not to come that way again.

"Jo, do you ever think about Daddy?"

She pauses, as if my question has surprised her. "All the time," she says softly. She looks down at Daddy's grave like he isn't there at all, but instead lives in her memory. Nobody talks much about him, probably because none of us is fond of crying. I envy Jo sometimes, mainly because she had more time with him. She was eighteen when he died. I had just turned twelve.

"Let's go home," Jo says, sliding her hand into mine. We lock fingers like best girlfriends.

"Goodbye, Daddy," I say, as we walk away.

Goodbye, Wildflower, I imagine him saying.

It takes nearly thirty minutes to get home. My secret way through the woods would have cut that time in half, but I'm not willing to tell anybody about it, not even Jo. Johnny is gone when we reach the crossroads, and my step lightens. I smile at the sky, imagining a world without Johnny Monroe.

Nearer to home the smell of honeysuckle and wild roses walks with us. As the sun dips below the ridge, the crickets warm up their night songs. Jo and I say our goodbyes at the three mailboxes at the bottom of our property. She and Daniel live across the road; Amy and Nathan next door to them. But there are several acres in between. I take the steep dirt path toward home, glad the rainstorm from the day before dampened down the dust from the dirt road.

To announce my arrival, I let the screen door slam. Mama and Meg are in the kitchen.

"Wash up," Mama says, and I do as I'm told.

Then I sit next to Meg who is still in her Woolworth's work clothes. Meg catches a ride to and from work with Cecil Appleby who drives his almost-new 1940 Ford truck into Rocky Bluff to work at the sock factory, an hour away. Not that many people have cars in Katy's Ridge.

"How's Daddy?" Meg asks.

"He's fine," I say. "He asked after you and I told him about your new job."

Meg smiles, but her smile has sadness in it, and I don't know if it's because she misses Daddy or if she's just sad she had to get a job.

Catching rides into Rocky Bluff makes a long day for Meg, because Cecil goes in at seven in the morning and she doesn't start work until nine. For two hours every morning she sits in the diner across from Woolworth's and reads cheap romance novels passed along by one of her customers.

Mama has no idea how much time Meg spends reading trashy novels and she would burn them in the woodstove if she ever found them. I have been sworn to secrecy until the day I die. However, not being one to pass up a business opportunity, I also collect ten cents a month for keeping my mouth shut. While Mama isn't looking, Meg slides me a dime across the table and I put it in my pocket.

A box under our bed is stacked full of books with bare-chested men standing next to women in long, sexy nightgowns. Meg says I can read them if I want to, but I can't get past the first chapter without feeling like heaving my breakfast oatmeal. If what's in those books is romance, I don't want any part of it.

In all my years of schooling, I've never had a boyfriend. I've had plenty of friends who were boys, but beyond that they hold no interest for me. In the country, some girls my age are already thinking about marriage. In the back, back woods, some girls are already having children of their own. But that's the last thing on my mind right now.

The secret sense tells me that Mama wants to say something to me about being at the graveyard again, but she swallows her words. If she wasn't so busy doing chores she might be up on that hill, too, lying next to Daddy's grave like they used to lie in bed together. I've never seen Mama cry, not even the day he died. But sometimes I hear her through the wall, tossing and turning all over the bed that doesn't have Daddy in it anymore.

"We waited supper on you," Mama says, as if this was a great inconvenience.

"Thank you, Mama," I say. Daddy would want me to be nice to her, even though she hasn't been that nice to me lately.

A large bowl of pinto beans sits on the kitchen table. We eat beans a lot since Daddy died. Mixed in with the beans are pieces of ham, sweet onion, and turnip greens—little surprises that your taste buds stumble upon. Mama places an iron skillet of cornbread just out of the oven on folded dishrags so it won't burn the wood. Next to the cornbread is a big plate of sliced tomatoes that Mama grows in the side yard. I spear three slices with my fork and put them on my plate. Then I remember how Mama always says my eyes are bigger than my stomach and put one back.

"Who came into the store today?" Mama asks Meg.

Meg starts naming names, most of which I recognize. You'd think Woolworth's was the center of our universe as much as they talk about it. The population of Rocky Bluff is roughly six hundred people. Katy's Ridge has all of eighty, five of which are my immediate family, and another dozen or so that are related in one way or another. Some of the markers in the graveyard date back to the 1840s, and there are at least a dozen confederate soldiers there, and two Union soldiers on the far side, a whole graveyard separating them. The 1860s saw a lot of funerals in Katy's Ridge. I can recite nearly every name and date on the tombstones, except the ones that are faded beyond recognition. Meg and Mama like to study the here and now. I like to study the past.

Mama rests her chin in her hand while Meg shares the latest gossip. Tonight's news consists of Marcy Trevor's new dentures that don't fit, even after paying a fancy dentist in Nashville, three hours away. Mama's eyebrows arch, as if hearing about Marcy's troubles gives her a break from her own.

While Mama soaks in the idle chatter, I sneak a third piece of cornbread, missing her speech on gluttony and how I won't always be skinny if I keep eating anything I want. Riled up, Mama can sound just like Preacher.

"Don't you have something to do?" Mama says to me. She doesn't wait for an answer.

I clear the table, a job I inherited after Amy left home. It is a chore I don't mind because I can let my mind wander while standing at the bucket in the kitchen sink. My thoughts travel old paths as well as new ones, depending on what we are studying in school or what I am reading. Pondering comes natural to me. I can sit and be entertained by my thoughts for enormous amounts of time. Mama calls this just being lazy.

I scrape the leftovers into a rusty pie tin to take out back to feed the stray cats that stay under our house. Daddy started this tradition, but Mama doesn't like it. She looks over at me and sighs.

"Your daddy was just too soft hearted with those cats," she says. "He would have attracted every stray cat in the state of Tennessee, if he'd had his way about it."

"Yes, Mama," I say. She says the same thing every night.

"You're lucky I don't drown them all," she says.

This threat is new and she looks at me as if to register the level of my shock. But I don't let my face tell her anything.

Not all the cats decide to stay, but the ones that do, run from Mama every time they see her. Even cats can sense when they're not wanted.

A new one showed up two days before, who is small and orange and doesn't mind being touched. On account of his color, I call him Pumpkin. I go outside and sit on the steps. Pumpkin finishes the little bits of food the other cats let him have and weaves between my ankles. As I rub his whiskers, he soaks up my attention with a raspy purr.

Even though I am full of Mama's cornbread and beans, I have a deep ache in my stomach when I think about Daddy being in the graveyard instead of sitting on the back porch with me. Evenings are the worst. It's the time of day when we all sat outside together. I lean against the porch post and close my eyes searching my memory for how his voice sounded.

A second later something rustles in the woods and I jump. The cats scatter, taking shelter under the house. Fixing my eyes on the woods, I wait for the next sound. Sometimes wild dogs roam the mountains, or raccoons come to eat what I've put out for the cats. I wrap my sweater closer and get that creepy feeling like when Johnny Monroe watches me.

"Who's out there?" I yell. My voice sounds shaky, so I stand to make up for it.

A million crickets answer my question.

Daddy's shotgun leans next to the back door, but Mama keeps the shells in her dresser drawer, so I'm not sure it would do much good to get it. By the time I got the gun loaded I could be dead and in a grave right next to his.

"Are you all right out here?" Mama says from behind the screen door. I've never been so glad to see her in all my life, but don't tell her that.

Even though I am nearly a woman myself, I am still a little girl in some ways. In the last year, I get scared by things that never used to scare me. It's as if my courage got buried along with Daddy.

"I heard something," I say, looking out into the woods.

Mama stands there for a long time, looking where I point.

"Come on inside," she says finally. The screen door needs grease and squeaks loudly as she opens it. After I pass, she latches it and the regular door, too, something I've never seen her do. Daniel put in the locks after Daddy died, but we've never once used them until now.

"What is it, Mama?" Meg asks. She yawns, as if realizing how long her day has already been.

"Louisa May heard something out back," Mama says.

She closes the short drapes over the kitchen sink, then walks through the living room and latches the front door, too. I like that she is taking me seriously for a change, but it also spooks me.

"Isn't it about time for you to get ready for bed?" Mama asks.

I glance at the clock and it's at least an hour before bed, so I figure she just wants me out of her hair. I leave Mama and Meg in the kitchen and sit in the rocker in the living room near the wood stove Daddy bought from the Sears & Roebuck catalog when I was seven. Daddy's banjo—missing one string he never got to replace—leans against the wall nearby. He used to sing country songs that told stories about people. His voice was deep and rich and it wrapped around you like one of Mama's softest quilts.

In the shadows, I pick up Daddy's old banjo and return to the rocker where he used to sit and play. I wrap his memory around me to try to feel safe. I am quiet, so Meg and Mama won't hear, and pretend to pick at some of the strings while I hum the words of *Down in the valley, valley so low*. At that moment the ache I felt earlier in my stomach moves to my chest. *Hang your head over, hear the wind blow.*

After I finish the song I get up from the rocking chair, being careful not to let it creak on the wooden floor. So Mama won't know I've touched it, I place Daddy's banjo back in its spot where the dust keeps the shape of it. It would be just like her to put it away if she knew I wanted to keep it out.

"What are you doing here in the dark?" Mama asks.

Speak of the devil, I start to say, but then think better of it.

Most of the things Mama says to me are either orders or questions, neither of which ever require an answer. I shrug and shuffle to the bedroom I share with Meg, who has already sunk into a loud snore. I get undressed and put on my nightgown and try not to think about the noise I heard earlier in the woods behind the house. When I walk down the hall toward Mama's room, I find her sitting on the edge of the bed brushing her hair, which reaches almost to her waist. Her hair is much prettier down, instead of up in the tight bun she wears during the day.

"Can I sleep with you?" I ask her. She looks at me surprised, like when I told her I was changing my name to Wildflower.

For a split second her face softens, but then she says, "Don't be silly, Louisa May. You're grown up now."

Her words sting like a bee stepped on barefooted in a patch of clover, and I want to kick myself for even asking. In my weakness, I imagined Mama opening the covers wide on Daddy's side of the bed while I get in.

Instead, she says, "Let me get at some of those tangles, Louisa May." She motions me over so she can brush my hair.

She starts and I say, "Ouch! Mama, stop!"

"Be still," she tells me, "you're just making my job harder."

While she attacks the tangles in my hair, I refuse to give her the pleasure of knowing how bad she's hurting me. Mama knows I'm tender-headed and I know she knows it. But it's as though I need her to touch me more than I need my pride, so I let her do it. In the meantime, I silently curse the tears that squeeze out of my eyes and promise myself that I'll be tougher once I turn thirteen.

After a while, Mama gives up and declares my tangles a battle she cannot win. Our eyes meet briefly before she turns away, as if the tangled emotions between us are also a losing battle.

I return to the bed I share with Meg. Lying there in the dark, I count backwards from a hundred by threes and try not to think about what's lurking in the woods or the fact that my father will never be coming home. Or my deepest, darkest, secret wish: that Mama had died instead of him.

CHAPTER TWO

The news of Ruby Monroe's death crackles through Katy's Ridge like an unexpected thunderstorm. The next morning, I overhear my sister Amy telling Mama about it in the kitchen. She must have come by early because she is already there when I wake up. Even though I am only days away from my thirteenth birthday, they never include me in their grownup conversations and sometimes I wonder if they ever will.

Squeezed behind the wood box full of kindling in the parlor, I slap at a cobweb that escaped Mama's dust rag. This was one of my many hiding places as a girl that can now barely accommodate me.

It is hot, as August always is, even early in the morning. A slender crack runs the length of the wall between the kitchen and the parlor, and I press my ear close to the wall in order to hear. It takes a few seconds to make out the words, but I tune them in like Daddy used to tune in stations on our old radio.

"Ruby hung herself," Amy says, her voice not much louder than a whisper.

I cover my mouth and swallow a gasp. I've heard of criminals getting hung, but I've never known anybody to do it to themselves. Especially somebody I just saw at Sweeny's store two days before. Ruby stood in front of the counter barefooted, her feet muddy, counting out pennies to Mr. Sweeny to buy a sack of flour. For all I knew she didn't even own shoes. Her stomach stuck out, like poor people's do, when they don't get enough to eat. I said hello and she nodded before quickly looking away.

After I inhale the dust of weathered oak from the wood box, a sneeze escapes. The muffled voices in the kitchen stop, as if wondering if a *bless you* is called for.

"Where's Louisa May?" Mama asks.

"She's still sleeping," Amy says.

Mama makes a comment about my laziness. At that moment I'm so riled up from being crammed in this hot, tight corner I fantasize about knocking some of Mama's spitefulness out of her.

"They found Ruby swinging in an oak tree," my sister, Amy, continues.

My eyes widen and I lean in closer, not wanting to miss a single detail.

"That poor child," Mama sighs.

"Her daddy came back from one of his hunting trips and found her," Amy says. "That's when he came to get Nathan. Nathan said Mr. Monroe was drunk, too, which didn't help matters. Melody was asleep in the house and Johnny was nowhere around."

Nathan is Amy's husband and one of the calmest human beings alive. He would be a good person to have around in an emergency.

"God rest her soul," Mama says.

"God rest her soul," Amy echoes.

"God rest her soul," I whisper.

Silence overtakes them. Wood dust works its way up my nose and I hold my breath and pinch my nostrils until the urge to sneeze again passes. If Mama catches me ease-dropping, I'll be cleaning the outhouse all afternoon.

"Nathan said it took two of them to cut her down," Amy says finally, her voice breaking.

When I close my eyes I can picture Ruby with her sad eyes and muddy feet, swinging by the neck from a tree she probably played in as a little girl. I feel sick at my stomach and have to remind myself to breathe.

"But I haven't told you the worst of it," Amy says, her words trailing off.

I press my ear into the narrow crack, certain I'll be rubbing out a crease later.

"What could be worse?" Mama asks.

I wonder the same.

"She was . . . in a family way," Amy whispers.

My breathing fills the silence as I imagine the looks they give each other. Mama can say more with her eyes than a whole dictionary full of words.

'In a family way' means Ruby's stomach wasn't just big from being hungry. As I lower my head, sweat drips onto my arm. Tears fill my eyes for Ruby Monroe and for her baby who will never see the light of day. The walls close in. I crawl from behind the wood box and tiptoe out the door, avoiding the floor boards I know will creak and step onto the porch. Fresh, warm air fills my lungs. Air, I am suddenly aware, Ruby will never get to breathe again.

Questions crowd my mind, as if sent to push the feelings away. Why would Ruby do such a thing? How could she possibly be so desperate and scared? And who is the father of her baby? I've never seen any boys around her. If this happened to me I wouldn't have to kill myself; Mama would do it for me.

Two days later, everybody in Katy's Ridge shows up for Ruby's funeral. The whispers are like a fire that refuses to die down and the packed church vibrates with judgment. The people of Katy's Ridge aren't all that forgiving when it comes to sinning. Meanwhile, Preacher's long face reveals what they already believe: the pearly gates of heaven won't be opening for the likes of Ruby Monroe.

Surely God won't send Ruby to hell just for having a hard life, I think. She didn't even own a pair of shoes and had to tend to a father and a brother who could have cared less about her. Preacher is fond of saying that the first will be last and the last first in God's kingdom. If this is true, then it makes more sense for God to send Ruby and her baby to the head of heaven's line.

Mama and I join Aunt Sadie, Daddy's older sister, and the rest of the family three rows from the front, the pew our family always sits in. The story told to me is that Ruby had an accident. But for the life of me I can't figure out how a rope could, by accident, slide around a person's neck.

I can't seem to take my eyes off of the wooden box that has Ruby in it. It smells of new lumber and hardly seems big enough for a thirteen year old girl and a baby and all the sadness she carried with her. I worry that she still doesn't have on any shoes and close my eyes to ask Daddy to put in a good word to God for Ruby and her baby.

"Have some respect for the dead," Mama whispers to me, as I lean over to get a better view. I want to remind her that I'm the one who spends a fair amount of time in the cemetery, not her, and if anybody has respect for the dead, that would be me.

Arthur Monroe sits on the front row wearing a torn pair of overalls, his dirty hat staying on his head the whole time. I've never seen him in church and he looks about as out of place as a mule in a kitchen. Johnny Monroe sits beside him, staring at the floor, his hair uncombed, with his younger sister, Melody, leaning into his arm. Melody's nose is running and she looks younger than her years. Her hair is tied up with a piece of knotted string.

The church is sweltering. It is three o'clock on an August afternoon with not a hint of breeze. Preacher clutches a worn, black Bible and bellows out the 23rd Psalm like we are all deaf or half-wits. Sweat forms in large half-moon circles under his arms. Droplets dance on his wide forehead as if the fires of hell are nipping at his dusty black shoes. He is bald except for a thin, sagging crescent of hair that reaches from one ear to the other, a temporary dam for the sweat, before it streams down his neck and forehead. To hear Preacher tell it, the whole of Katy's Ridge is doomed to teeth gnashing with the devil because of all the hearty sinning we do.

His face flushes crimson. His voice raised, he speaks of God calling his children home when they least expect it. He shouts "Repent!" several times and warns us to not end up like Ruby. Johnny hasn't looked up once, not even with Preacher standing a foot away from him. If I was a betting person, I'd bet Johnny wishes he had a peach can to sit at Preacher's feet to ping some tobacco spit into.

The top of a whiskey bottle bulges out of Mr. Monroe's pocket and on one of Preacher's *repents* Mr. Monroe snarls and takes out his pocketknife. He opens the blade swiftly with his thumb and scrapes at the dirt caked on the bottom of his boots, letting the dirt fall onto the church floor. Two deacons start to come forward to take Mr. Monroe out of the church but Preacher holds up a hand to stop them, as if even he knows this wouldn't turn out well.

Mr. Monroe doesn't look the least bit sorry for Ruby's death and heat rises to my face. I want to smack the man from here to Christmas, and Preacher, too, whose empty words make no sense. Why would God call Ruby home by way of a rope and an oak tree? A trickle of sweat slides between my shoulder blades and I let out a huff. If God decides to call me home anytime soon, I will refuse to answer.

Arthur Monroe's livelihood is hunting, setting traps and selling the meat. His clothes always stink like a ripe carcass. Though he is an eligible widower, his odor discourages even the most ardent widows and spinsters of Katy's Ridge.

If he manages to corner you anywhere, on the road, or at Sweeny's store, he'll tell you the story of getting gassed in a trench in the big war in Europe, World War I, and the whole time you're getting gassed just standing there. On one of those occasions when I was wishing I had a gas mask, Mr. Monroe told me that once or twice a year he checks into the Veterans Hospital in Nashville with blinding headaches. I got a headache just hearing about it.

A few years ago, during one of those headaches, he came after Johnny at school for forgetting to feed Arthur's old coon dog. The whole school witnessed him bursting through the door and dragging Johnny right out into the schoolyard. While he beat the tar out of him, he kept yelling, "Get behind me, Satan!" A short time after that, Johnny quit coming to school and started hanging out on the road.

Sweat sticks my legs to the wooden bench. I think of Ruby inside that box, her baby inside of her, Ruby's belly being its own little casket. It is entirely possible that I have entered my own version of hell where life is not fair and the wrong people die and for no good reason.

Mama takes my pinkie finger on my right hand and bends it to the point of pain. This is my signal to stop my squirming in church. As I take my hand away, I give her a look that says she will end up like Ruby if she's not careful and she gives me a look back as if daring me to try it. Meanwhile, Preacher is using Ruby's death to put the fear of God in us and further his cause. After Preacher finishes, he looks pleased with himself and wipes the sweat from his face with a starched white handkerchief and looks over at the organ.

In a flourish of wrong notes, Miss Mildred starts playing *Amazing Grace*, real slow. This was Daddy's favorite hymn, but I try not to think about that, or about the last time I heard it, which was at his funeral. We all sing along, most of the congregation confident that Ruby Monroe was the wretch that needed saving in the first verse and since she never came to church she was out of luck. Ruby was lost, but nobody even tried to find her.

When the music stops, the four McClure brothers go up front to lift Ruby's pine box to carry it to the gravesite. Buddy, the youngest McClure, grunts as if the box weighs more than he expects. They balance their load and we file out of the church, following the box up the hill. In the distance a pile of fresh red dirt marks Ruby's final resting place, a stone's throw away from Daddy's willow tree.

A fine, misty rain starts to fall and the melody of *Amazing Grace* still plays in my head while we walk up the hill. Aunt Sadie lightly squeezes my hand and I have the secret sense that she knows exactly what I am thinking about. The last time we climbed this hill was nearly a year ago.

"Are you okay, sweetheart?" Aunt Sadie asks, and I say, *yes,* though I'm not the least bit okay. Now I have proof that God doesn't know what he's doing by taking both Daddy and Ruby before their time.

Ruby's box is lowered into the grave with two ropes and Preacher throws a clump of muddy red dirt into the hole. The dirt hits Ruby's coffin with a dull thud and Mama jerks her head like a gun has gone off, and then she glances off into the distance at Daddy's grave. As far as I know, she hasn't visited it once since Daddy died, and I want to take her by the hand and lead her there and show her how beautiful the spot is. But her eyes are as ominous and blue gray as the sky.

"Ashes to ashes, dust to dust," Preacher says and the words sound hollow.

When someone your same age dies, it's like it could have been you. I hope I never get as desperate and sad as Ruby. Losing my father taught me how deep sadness can go. The rain grows harder and thunder rumbles in the distance. Another summer storm passes through Katy's Ridge as we say our goodbyes to Ruby Monroe.

CHAPTER THREE

When I tell Daniel and Nathan I heard somebody in the woods three nights before, they come by and search the hill behind our house.

"We saw deer tracks," Daniel says, when they return to the back porch. He stomps the mud from his boots on the top step, then uses the side of his boot to sweep the mud away. Daniel looks over at me and shrugs his shoulders in an apology, like he wishes he'd found something.

"It was just Louisa May's imagination getting the best of her," Mama says. "She's been like that since she was a little girl."

Her words make me doubly mad. For one thing she refuses to call me Wildflower, and for another she acts like I don't know the difference between my imagination and something real in the woods. That was no deer that night, I am certain of it. I've been around plenty of deer, and a deer in the woods doesn't make my skin crawl.

Meg comes home from work, fixes herself a glass of tea and joins us.

"What's going on?" Meg asks.

"A wild goose chase, that's what," Mama says.

Daniel puts a hand on my shoulder as if to discourage me from wrestling Mama to the ground.

"You've got a nest of baby possums in the base of that old Hickory," Nathan says, hitching up his pants. He is as lean as the fence rails he put around his field last summer and has to wear both a belt and suspenders. People joke with Amy that she doesn't feed her husband near enough, but I've seen him put away as much food as two regular sized men.

"Are you sure you heard something?" Daniel asks me. He keeps his arm on my shoulder. I am just the right height for Daniel to use as an armrest.

"I'm sure," I say. If anybody else had asked, I'd probably gotten madder still. But Daniel doesn't ask it like he thinks I am somebody who just makes things up.

"Sometimes the wind in the trees makes some weird rustling. It even fools me," he says.

"I know what I heard, Daniel," I say. "It was too heavy-footed for a deer or the wind. It was a person, I'm sure of it. Mama says it was just my imagination but she felt creepy about it, too. She locked up the house tighter than a drum."

Mama looks at me like I've somehow made a liar out of her. I scowl at Meg, leaving space for her to side with me, but she doesn't say a word.

"Who'd be traipsing around in these woods?" Nathan asks.

"I bet I know," I say, regretting the words the moment I speak them. Mama looks at me all curious. This is not a road I want to take. The less information Mama knows the better.

"What did you say?" she asks.

I stick my hands deep into the pockets of my overalls and finger a smooth, round stone I fished out of the streambed the day before. Rocks aren't supposed to interest girls my age, so I hide my treasures now.

"I said I know who it was," I say again, but I sound more timid this time.

Everybody looks at me like I am Moses about to deliver the Ten Commandments. Mama folds her arms into her chest, her lips tight. When I was younger, this could make the truth spill out of me like cornmeal out of a sack. But I am not in the mood to give her what she wants.

"Well, who was it?" Mama asks. "Those baby possums out back have already had time to be weaned and have babies of their own."

Everybody waits while I debate which of my actions will get me in the least amount of trouble. If I tell, Mama will be like a dog given a new bone to chew on. If I don't, Johnny might just walk right into our house someday like he owns the place.

"It was Johnny Monroe, that's who it was," I say finally.

Daniel takes his arm off my shoulder. He places his foot on the porch rail and leans on his knee, as if this information changes things.

"Johnny's a good-for-nothin', that's for sure," Nathan says.

Johnny is Nathan's second cousin, but they aren't close. Practically everybody in their family has given up on Johnny. He is what people around here call a "black sheep."

"It was him," I insist.

Mama presses her fingers into her temples like I am giving her one whopper of a headache.

"I wouldn't put it past him," Daniel says. "Those Monroes know these mountains better than anybody. They might be watching us right now."

"But why would Johnny come up here?" Mama asks. Her eyes narrow like she's just set a trap for me.

I mumble that I don't know and shoot Meg a look that threatens to expose her entire collection of romance novels under our bed. Meg doesn't flinch from my threat and pours herself another glass of tea.

I am not about to tell Mama how many times Johnny has asked after Meg, or the things Johnny has said to me. She'll make too big of a deal about it or no deal at all. But it would be just like Johnny to hike up the ridge and perch on the hillside in the hopes of getting a look at Meg or me in our underwear.

"We could go ask Johnny about it," Daniel says to Mama.

"No, you boys have done enough," Mama says. "I'm sure it's nothing to fuss about." She goes into the pantry and gets them each a jar of homemade applesauce. Mama never lets anybody leave the house without giving them something to take back home. Applesauce, apples, tomatoes, strawberry preserves—anything she has extra in the pantry. "Tell the girls I said hello," Mama says.

They each kiss Mama on the cheek.

"The best part of having grown daughters is the sons-in-law that come with them," Mama says.

She looks over at Meg and me like she expects us to come up with someone to marry who is just as good. I don't know how to tell her that I have no interest whatsoever. All girls want to do around here when they grow up is get married. But if I can't find somebody as good as Daddy, I'm not going to bother.

Later that night Meg and I are in bed and I give her the silent treatment because I am still fuming that she didn't speak up earlier about what I heard in the woods.

"Johnny gives me the creeps, too," Meg says. She turns a page of her book.

"Really?" I ask, my anger turning to relief.

"Just stay away from him," she says, not looking up.

"I do stay away from him," I say, "except when he's waiting on the road. But what if that was him out back the other night, Meg?"

She puts a finger in the book to mark her place and turns to face me. "Johnny's too lazy to come all the way up here. He hangs out mainly on the road. It was probably a deer or something and you just imagined it was Johnny."

It feels like the hundredth time that day my grasp on reality has been questioned, but I am just too tired to argue.

"I'll turn out the light in a minute," she says. Meg moistens her bottom lip with her tongue like she is reading something delicious, and then turns another page.

According to Preacher, God is real big on forgiveness, especially for us lowly sinners like Meg who has a fondness for romance novels. With that in mind, I decide to forgive Meg, too, though I'm not about to give Preacher credit for it.

I close my eyes and pray for Meg to find someone to love soon so she will quit reading romances and go to bed at a decent hour. She pretends to be happy that Jo and Amy got married last spring, but I know she's jealous and wants someone of her own.

The house is quiet. While she's reading, Meg always keeps one eye on the door in case Mama comes in so she can throw her book under the covers. But Mama has gone to bed early with a headache. A headache she probably blames on me.

I think about Daddy resting in peace on the hillside, the moonlight dancing with the breeze through the weeping willow tree.

"Goodnight, Daddy," I whisper.

Sleep well, Wildflower, he whispers back.

CHAPTER FOUR

On my thirteenth birthday I have cramps so bad I can barely stand. This is my fourth monthly and I am still getting used to the whole thing. Growing up with older sisters has its advantages. It wasn't a mystery for me. When it happened, Mama gave me two cotton pads she had sewn together out of leftover quilt pieces. One I wear inside my underpants. The other I use as a spare when I wash the soiled one out in the evenings. Mama made each of us different colored pads so we could tell them apart. Mine are white, with pieces of light blue running through. With all these girls and Mama, there are times when the back clothesline will have a whole bunch of pads hanging on it, like flags from different countries.

"Come on, Wildflower, open your presents," Daniel says. He motions for me to sit on the porch and everybody else gathers around.

We're all full of Mama's chicken and dumplings she made me for my birthday dinner and are moving kind of slow. Jo baked a cake that we will dig into after presents.

Meg hands me a small package wrapped in paper from the Sunday funnies and some twine. I open it and find a comb and mirror that all fit together in a little leather pouch from the Woolworth store. I thank her and give her a hug. I love the gifts she's given me since she started working there.

Amy and Nathan's package is much bigger and contains a new dress to wear to church. It is red with a small white daisy pattern. It also has two big pockets on the front because Amy knows I like collecting things.

"Thanks, Amy," I say.

"I know you like red," Amy says, "and daisies are also wildflowers, just like your name."

I appreciate how thoughtful her gift is and tell her so. Amy sews better than anybody in Katy's Ridge and a lot of women pay her to make them things they see in the Sears & Roebuck catalog. The extra money really helps out since Nathan's crops depend on how good the weather is and it isn't always good.

"Here's a little something extra," Nathan says, hitching up his pants for the hundredth time. He hands me a corncob pipe and everybody laughs. "You're old enough now to start up smoking any day," Nathan adds.

I laugh, too, though I'm not feeling that festive.

But then Mama chimes in, "She'd better not ever smoke," and all the laughter stops.

Next to give presents are Daniel and Jo. Daniel hands me a carved wooden box he whittled that has a small wooden cat inside. Both are beautiful and I thank him and Jo for such a perfect gift.

"My turn," Aunt Sadie says. She hands me a present wrapped in fabric with wildflowers stitched on front that is beautiful enough to be the gift itself. Inside is a little book with blank paper in it to write down my pondering thoughts. Only Aunt Sadie would think of something like that. She also brought me some herbs for my cramps, without me even asking; like she had the secret sense that I needed them.

Sadie gives me a big hug and whispers in my ear, "He's looking down on you right now, sweetheart, and he's very proud."

Her words bring tears to my eyes that I brush away as quick as they land on my cheeks.

Aunt Sadie is Daddy's older sister by sixteen years. She took care of him back in Ireland when he was a baby, while their parents worked. She often tells me that I remind her of herself as a girl. She says I have gumption. I'm not sure what 'gumption' is but I take it as a compliment.

Aunt Sadie likes telling the story of how she came to America on her own when she turned twenty-two. Daddy came two years later after Grandpa McAllister died. I asked her once why she decided to settle in Katy's Ridge because it seems to me there would have been much more exciting places to live. She said the Tennessee mountains reminded her of home.

None of my grandparents are still alive, but Aunt Sadie comes closest to being a grandmother to me. She has solid white hair and sometimes uses a walking stick with a tree carved on the side. Not that she is the least bit feeble. It just helps to steady her when she climbs the mountain looking for the plants she needs for her remedies, especially the ginseng, hiding out on damp, shady hillsides. Her dog, Max, always goes with her and carries a leather pouch on his back for collecting the plants and roots Sadie finds. Max and I are friends, too, and whenever I go over to Sadie's house he lets me pick cockleburs out of his fur and brush him.

Today, Max is lying on the end of the porch sleeping. Every now and again he opens his eyes to make sure Sadie is where he left her.

Everybody makes a big deal of my birthday, probably because they know how hard it is to not have Daddy here. Next month marks the one-year-anniversary of his death. Earlier that day at the cemetery, I told God that I'd settle for no presents for the rest of my life if Daddy could just come home one more time. As a result, I keep glancing down the hill, half-expecting to see him coming home from work, whistling and walking with his familiar gait.

Jo goes inside and in a few seconds brings out the cake she made. We will eat it on the front porch so the crumbs won't get everywhere in the house. Everybody knows how Mama fusses over the house and nobody wants to make her mad.

"Make a wish," Jo says. She lights a single candle in the center of the cake, the same candle we all use for birthdays, kept in the kitchen drawer with the twine and matches.

While everyone watches, I exaggerate a big breath and blow out the candle. Then everybody claps and I glance down the hill to see if my wish has come true. My shoulders drop with the knowledge that I probably won't get my wish of seeing Daddy again until the day I don't have birthdays anymore.

In the meantime, Daniel and Nathan eat big slices of cake with their hands. They make noises like it's the best they've ever tasted. The rest of us have forks and plates, but make the same sounds. It is vanilla cake with vanilla frosting and coconut resting on top like the first snow of winter. The taste is heavenly, which makes me wonder if there is food in heaven. The next time I sit with Daddy in the graveyard I'll have to ask.

After we finish our cake, Mama asks, "So when is Mary Jane coming home, Louisa May?"

I've told her twice already, but it isn't like her to make conversation with me, so I figure, along with the chicken and dumplings, this must be part of my birthday present.

"She won't be home till the first of September," I say.

Mary Jane and I have been inseparable since we were babies and our mother's laid us on a blanket together in Pritchard's Meadow on the 4th of July.

"Oh, that's right," she says. "I think you told me that before."

With a glance, I suggest she ask me something else, since she had already asked the previous question, but our conversation stops there. If Daddy were here he would joke her out of her grumpiness and have her smiling and hanging on his arm in no time. Wishing for a miracle, I glance down the hill again.

Mary Jane always misses my August birthday because every summer she goes to Little Rock, Arkansas, on a Greyhound bus. If not for Mary Jane I'd be friendless. A year ago, I used to have more friends, but then after Daddy died they acted like they didn't know what to say to me. Mountain people are superstitious, especially about accidents. I think they stay away so they won't get any bad luck on them.

Sometimes Mary Jane goes with me to the graveyard to visit Daddy. She has a couple of uncles there and a grandfather. Whenever we visit she says hello to them, but mostly she just goes to keep

me company. Most other girls I know get squeamish about graveyards and tombstones, but not Mary Jane. Dead people don't bother
her.

While my family sits on the front porch looking full and content,
Amy gets Nathan a second slice of cake. Before the night is over he'll
probably get thirds and fourths. Jo and Daniel hold hands in the
porch swing that Daddy made. Mama and Aunt Sadie pull out the
quilt they've been working on since last Christmas, made out of the
scraps of our old clothes. They are good at making something beautiful out of scraps.

As I lean against the porch, I break a stick into knuckle-sized
pieces and corral an ant carrying a piece of coconut across the porch
rail. The ant keeps hitting against the wall I've created and I feel bad
for making its life harder. But in a way it feels like what God has
done to me by letting my father die.

Forgetting all about my promise to be tough when I turn thirteen, I start to tear up again. It occurs to me that all this emotion
might be from having my monthly, given Jo cries at the sight of a
hummingbird when she has hers.

After excusing myself, I meander around back to give Pumpkin
some of my cake crumbs. I have to shoo off the other cats. From
the ice box, I steal her a tiny bit of cream, hoping mama won't miss
it. *Cream is not to be wasted on cats,* she has said more than once.

Pumpkin and I sit on the back porch and watch the last rays of
sunlight stream through the trees. It will be dark soon. Lightning
bugs blink in the forest like tiny stars come to earth.

My thoughts keep me company as Pumpkin finishes off the last
of the cream and begins an extensive cleaning ritual. Thirteen feels
old to me. I'll graduate from grade school this year. Not everybody

who goes to our grade school goes to high school, too. But Daddy wanted all of us McAllisters to get our high school diplomas so I'll be going to Rocky Bluff High School next year. Meg was the smartest in her class and even gave the commencement speech last June, so it is doubly hard to understand her fascination for tawdry novels.

The grade school in Katy's Ridge had a total of twelve students of various ages. We meet in one big room with a coal stove in the center. A big pile of coal sits out back and we kids take turns going to get a piece to throw in the stove in the winter. Beyond the coal pile we have a field where we play kickball every day after lunch. In contrast, Rocky Bluff High School has nearly a hundred students and more classrooms than I've taken the time to count.

To get to the high school from Katy's Ridge, I will have to walk a mile down the river road to catch an old Rocky Bluff city bus that comes only a little ways into Katy's Ridge. After the weather gets cold, Meg says the buses are freezing and you can see your breath out in front of you. Then you hardly warm up before you have to get back on the cold bus again and head home. On the coldest winter days I plan to wear my overalls under my dress and take them off once I get to school.

From my pocket, I take out Mary Jane's letter that came yesterday. She will be home next week. I can't wait to show her the things I got for my birthday, and tell her about Ruby Monroe, and about hearing something in the woods behind our house. In her letter she said her grandmother bought her some dresses at the J.C. Penney store in downtown Little Rock. Mary Jane sent me pictures she tore out of the J.C. Penney catalog and I look at them again, thinking they must look like something Shirley Temple wears. I have never owned a store bought dress in my life.

"There you are," Daniel says. He walks around the side of the house and sits next to me on the back porch. "Why'd you leave the party?"

I shrug and Daniel nods like I've given a perfectly good reason. For several seconds the two of us share a duet of silence. Then I notice my pad from yesterday hanging on the clothesline and think, *God in Heaven!* I flush hot from something so private being all exposed. But Daniel doesn't even notice. Or if he does, he doesn't let on.

Pumpkin weaves between our legs. Daniel is the only other human, besides me, he will get close to.

"Thanks for the carving," I say. I pull the wooden cat out of my pocket and admire it for his benefit. I left the wooden box on the porch with my other things.

"I thought you'd like it," he says. "The wood came from the mill. It's oak. It'll last forever." He smiles and looks proud that he's made me happy. Two years before, Daddy got Daniel a job at the sawmill. They used to walk there together every morning.

We sit quietly, watching Pumpkin spear the last piece of coconut on the plate with one claw. He nibbles it down.

"A penny for your thoughts," Daniel finally says.

Maybe my thoughts aren't even worth a penny, I don't know. But I feel like asking for at least a quarter. Grief, I decide, comes at great expense. I shrug again and ponder how the sadness of losing somebody you love never goes away. It just fades over the years like the pattern on a dress that's been passed down.

"Well, whenever you want to talk about it, I'm here," Daniel says.

I smile, remembering how much Daniel reminds me of Daddy sometimes.

"I can't believe I'm thirteen," I say finally. "It's the oldest I've ever been."

Daniel chuckles, but stops himself when he sees I am being serious.

I spit on my fingers to wipe a streak of mud from my shoes. Truth is I'm not so sure I want to share what I've been thinking. But when I look over at Daniel I know I can trust him to understand.

"Daddy had all these plans for my thirteenth birthday, on account of me becoming a teenager," I say. "He promised to take me on the train to Nashville and visit the state capital."

Daniel pauses. "You still miss him don't you," he says.

"More than anything," I say softly.

"He was a good man," Daniel says, his voice low, matching mine. "I miss him, too."

I tell myself not to cry, that I'm being ridiculous, and the voice in my head sounds a lot like Mama. I choke back the tears that want to pour out over the front of my dress, over Pumpkin, then all the way past the graveyard, and out to the river to the sea.

Daniel puts his arm around me. The scent of sweat and sawdust reminds me even more of what I'm missing. Tears stream from my eyes. I bury my head in the skirt of the dress that Meg handed down to me after it was Amy's before it was Jo's. We McAllisters usually don't let anybody see us cry, even family, unless something really bad happens.

"It's okay," Daniel says. "There's nobody here to see but God and some crickets."

For the next few minutes I make a friend of my misery imagining how my life could have been different: Daddy here celebrating my 13th birthday with me, playing his banjo on the front porch with everybody dancing and laughing; Daddy looking over at me, smiling, like he's the luckiest man alive to have me as a daughter. Then afterwards we would catch a ride to Rocky Bluff and take the train to Nashville.

These thoughts serve no purpose but to torture me. Meanwhile, Daniel has his arm around me, waiting for the unexpected cloudburst of tears to stop. It feels good to have a man's arm around me, even if he isn't the man I really want.

"Hey you two," Jo says, coming around the corner of the house. She hesitates when she sees me crying, but then keeps coming. Every time I see Jo she gets more beautiful, like those girls in magazines advertising Ivory soap.

"Am I interrupting?" she asks Daniel, resting a hand on his shoulder.

"We've just been reminiscing," he says.

"Do you need more time?" Jo says, stroking my hair.

"No," I say.

I wipe my face on the underside of my dress, and tell myself to snap out of it, that I am not a little girl any more. Again, the voice sounds more like mama's than mine, but it serves its purpose.

"Let's get back to the party," I say, standing up to leave. When I move, Pumpkin runs behind the old washing machine.

Jo hugs me gently, like I am a flower whose blossom might collapse if touched. Jo is my favorite sister, even though I love them all.

"We've got another surprise for you," she says, smiling at Daniel.

"What is it?" I ask. I prefer good news to bad any day.

"We want to tell everybody all at once," Daniel says. He takes Jo's hand and the three of us follow the path back around the house lined with the rock Daddy and I carried from the river.

Mama is still in her rocking chair with pieces of quilt stretched between her and Aunt Sadie. Nathan balances on the porch rail picking his teeth with a twig he's whittled down, while Amy pours more tea for everybody. Max is asleep at Aunt Sadie's feet. He is the dog version of an old man and doesn't trouble himself with much except watching out for Aunt Sadie.

"It's about time you showed up," Mama says to me. She looks up briefly from her stitching. "What kind of girl disappears from her own party?"

"A beautiful girl," Aunt Sadie says, as if trying to make up for the softness Mama lacks since Daddy died.

I sit on the porch steps and refuse to let Mama ruin my birthday. Torches are lit now that it's getting dark.

"Jo and I have an announcement to make," Daniel says, standing in the middle of the dirt yard.

Amy grins and looks over at Jo like she already knows what it is, and Meg wears that moony look she gets whenever she reads romance stories. Everybody seems to know what Daniel is going to say except me.

"What is it?" I ask, the suspense nudging me from all directions.

"I'm going to have a baby," Jo smiles.

I should have guessed this is what she was going to say. She is more radiant than I've ever seen her.

Everybody converges on Jo and Daniel, laughing and hugging Jo and patting Daniel on the back. Meanwhile, I sit frozen, like somebody has nailed my backside to the porch steps. Unexpected things throw me these days, even if they are good things.

"If it's a boy we're going to name him Joseph, after Daddy," Jo says. "And if it's a girl, we'll call her Penelope."

Mama rises from her rocker, puts the quilt aside and embraces Jo and Daniel. Penelope is Mama's given name, even though Daddy always called her Nell. Only Sadie calls her Nell now, along with a few people at church. I keep forgetting she has a name besides "Mama."

Aunt Sadie tip-toes into the yard, her arms raised high in the air and starts to dance. Max barks excitedly. Aunt Sadie has been known to dance whenever the spirit moves her. Preacher hates it when the spirit comes over Aunt Sadie in church. Sadie's dancing always sparks a sermon from Preacher about how the "heathens" are taking over the world. To me, it looks like God would want people to dance and celebrate life like that.

The celebration continues around me. I try my best to get excited about Daniel and Jo's news but all I can think about is Daddy missing this moment, and how proud he'd be about having his first grandchild.

"You're going to be an aunt," Daniel says to me, a big grin on his face.

"Congratulations," I say, smiling back. I like the idea of being an aunt, like Aunt Sadie. If Daniel and Jo have a boy, I'll teach him how to use a slingshot and maybe play the banjo. If it is a girl, I'll do my best to teach her how to stay clear of Johnny Monroe.

Jo walks over and gives me another hug. "We thought this would make your thirteenth birthday even more special," she says.

I manage a smile, not wanting to get any of my sadness on the baby. What bothers me most is the thought that life just keeps on going, even when somebody you love dies. Another McAllister is going to be born into the world, one Daddy will never know.

CHAPTER FIVE

"Well, if it isn't my best friend in the whole wide world, Wild-flower McAllister," Mary Jane says when she first sees me again. I can tell she's trying to sound more grown up than she was two months ago when I last saw her.

I always forget how red Mary Jane's hair is until she comes home. She is the only person in Katy's Ridge with this distinction. Neither of her parents have red hair, which raises the eyebrows of the old ladies at church when they don't have anything better to gossip about. Not everybody remembers that Mary Jane's grandmother's hair used to be red, before it turned solid gray.

"It's about time you got home," I say. "Katy's Ridge is the most boring place on earth without you."

Mary Jane and I are always trying to outdo each other by talking grand.

"I thought I'd keel over and die without you!" Mary Jane says.

I roll my eyes, calling a halt to the contest.

Mary Jane also has more freckles on her face than all the people in Katy's Ridge combined. One day last year we started counting them during recess and got up to 84 before we had to go back inside. People expect her to have a fiery temper, too, but in all the years I've known her I've never seen even a hint of one. If anything, I should have red hair instead of her.

We spend the whole morning in Mary Jane's room and she shows me her new school clothes. Preacher says coveting is a sin. Coveting has to do with wanting what other people have, like their land, their wives or mules. I figure this goes for new dresses, too, even though I'd much prefer a new pair of overalls.

Amy makes everything we McAllister's wear and she makes them sturdy—dresses and pants alike. But when it comes to the day-to-day living of life, dresses just aren't practical. Bare legs attract all sorts of annoying things like cuts, scrapes and bug bites. Not to mention that every time I take a notion to swing in grade school, boys try to sneak a peek at my underpants.

Meg says high school boy's eyes wander more to the top part of a girl than the bottom and since I don't have much to show in that department, I should be fine. At least I've had practice with Johnny Monroe.

"Look at this one," Mary Jane says. She takes a dress out of a J.C. Penney box and drapes it across her arm like it is a mink stole.

"That must have cost a fortune," I say.

"How about two fortunes," Mary Jane says.

I lie across Mary Jane's bed, finding it impossible not to covet the J.C. Penney dress before me. It is green plaid and looks like something Katherine Hepburn might wear. I promise myself that the next time I visit the graveyard I will send God, by way of Daddy, my apologies for this latest weakness of mine.

"Grandma also bought me these," Mary Jane says.

I gasp when Mary Jane brings out a brand new box of colored pencils and a pad of drawing paper. I have never in my life owned a box of colored pencils. At best, I've inherited broken crayon stubs, previously used by Jo, Amy, and Meg, kept in an old cigar box. Temptation grows stronger and I feel a sin coming on. Not coveting Mary Jane's new art supplies is much harder than not coveting her dresses and seems an unfair challenge for God to throw at me.

Thou shalt not covet thy friend's art supplies, may very well be the hardest commandment of all.

Think of all the pictures those colored pencils could make, with their perfectly sharpened tips. This temptation, as Preacher would be happy to point out, puts me right in my very own Garden of Eden talking to the snake. A snake that has every intention of getting me to bite into that apple. Truth be told, I would not hesitate to take a hefty bite out of that wicked fruit if promised art supplies. A fact, of which, I am not particularly proud.

"So what have you been doing all summer?" Mary Jane asks.

"Staying clear of Johnny Monroe, mainly," I say.

"He's disgusting," she says. She uses her hands to smooth some of the creases in the dress.

"Disgusting just about sums it up," I say.

"None of the boys in Katy's Ridge are even worth looking at," she says for about the hundredth time. "However, Little Rock is full of cute boys."

I listen for the next thirty minutes to Mary Jane describe different boys in Little Rock, Arkansas. Her report is so titillating, I start to doze off.

"So have you been to the graveyard lately?" she asks, at the end of her litany.

Her question startles me awake.

"Nearly every day," I say.

Mary Jane is the only person in the world who knows why visiting Daddy is important to me: I'm afraid I'll forget him. The longer he's dead, the more I play moving pictures of him in my mind, anchoring his memory in place.

Just this morning I remembered how when I was a little girl I'd pretend to shave with him. I played that memory over and over in my mind like I was memorizing a poem for school, except this poem wasn't words but images. I'd use a stick as a razor, imitating him while he stood on the front porch. During the warmer months he always shaved squinting into a tiny mirror tacked up on the house. A basin of soapy water collected the tiny whiskers until he threw it out into the ivy underneath the pine tree beside the porch. He told me that whiskers would grow like pole beans under that pine, and for years I believed him, but they never did.

"I think I'll wear this one the first day back to school," Mary Jane says. She holds up a yellow dress with a green belt. She admires it, her hands on her hips. Unlike me, Mary Jane has filled out instead of up.

"I got a new dress for my birthday," I say. "Amy sewed it."

"Amy's the best seamstress in Katy's Ridge," she says. "Anything she makes is much nicer than these store bought things."

Mary Jane probably knows that if she ever rubs it in about how much more she has than me, we wouldn't be friends. Her grandmother in Little Rock is rich and both my grandmothers are dead. My grandmother on my mother's side died before I was born and the one from my father's side died when I was five. Not to mention that with Daddy gone we barely have any money at all. The government sends Mama a little, but the rest she makes up by selling things in Rocky Bluff like quilts and canned jams and jellies.

Most of the time, I can be happy about Mary Jane's good fortune. But lately, since my birthday, at least, I've felt sorry for myself and thought more about what I don't have instead of what I do.

"Well, hello Louisa May. Did you have a nice summer?" Mary Jane's mother doesn't look at me but admires the dresses spread out across the room.

"Yes, ma'am," I say, wondering why grownups always ask questions instead of talking to you like a normal person.

Even when she's relaxed, Mary Jane's mom stands rigid like she has a board strapped to her back and looks taller than most women. Mary Jane is so short you'd never think that they were even related. In my family, Meg and Amy look just like Mama and people say I look just like Daddy. Jo doesn't look like anybody, except maybe a movie star. And as far as I can tell, Mary Jane doesn't look like anybody, either, except maybe her grandmother.

"Louisa May, would you like to stay for dinner?" Mary Jane's mother asks.

Mary Jane and I smile at each other like life is good and just got better. "Yes, ma'am," I say. "But I'll need to ask first."

"That's fine," she says. She walks over and smoothes the creases of Mary Jane's new dress with one of her hands. I see the family resemblance in her actions. "Maybe Louisa May would like some of your older dresses, dear," she says to Mary Jane before she leaves, as if it has suddenly occurred to her to have pity on me.

Mary Jane's eyes widen and she looks over at me like I might take a swing at her own mother. She knows I hate being pitied. But instead of reacting, I take a deep breath and sit on my hands. I've faced enough temptation for one day.

According to Preacher, Jesus wants us to turn the other cheek when someone insults us, so I say, "No thank you, ma'am," and bite my lip to keep from smiting Mary Jane's kin.

Given the sheer number of church potlucks we've all attended over the years, it is a well-known fact that Mary Jane's mother can't cook nearly as well as mine. But her family always eats off fancy dishes that have ivy leaves painted all around the edges and were made in China. I also like that Mary Jane has a father sitting at the table, which reminds me of how my family used to be.

Mary Jane and I walk down the road to tell Mama I won't be home for dinner. We are good at moseying and set out to do just that. I already dread the thought of seeing Johnny Monroe on the road and wish we had a telephone so we could just call instead of walk the mile to my house.

Mary Jane's parents own the only telephone in Katy's Ridge. If anybody needs help they go there to call the ambulance in Rocky Bluff. Otherwise, they go to Doc Lester, who isn't really a doctor, but went to veterinary school for a year and still has all the books. Doc Lester smells funny, a sickly combination of rubbing alcohol, hair tonic and cow manure.

It is hot for September and the dirt from the road sticks to our legs as we walk. Mary Jane and I take turns swatting horse flies that love to drink the salty sweat from the creases of our elbows and knees.

We come to the crossroad, about halfway between our two houses, and there stands Johnny Monroe, kicking up the dirt with his scuffed up boots.

"Well, look who's here," Johnny says. "Twiddle Dee and Twiddle Dum." He gives the dirt an extra kick.

Though I am already staring at my shoes, this statement almost prompts me to look up. Not because I am insulted, but because it amazes me that Johnny has ever read a book, especially *Alice in Wonderland*. I decide he must have heard someone else say it.

"What do we do?" Mary Jane whispers to me. She matches my stance, lowering her head and hunching her shoulders since she actually has something to hide.

"Just keep walking and don't say anything," I whisper back.

Since Mary Jane doesn't have to pass this way to go to school, she hasn't had as many dealings with Johnny as I have.

"You girls want to go into the woods and have a little fun?" Johnny laughs.

Something in the way he laughs makes me look up just long enough to see a trickle of brown juice from Johnny's tobacco chew running down his chin. My half-digested lunch quickly rises from my stomach and lodges in my throat. I taste parts of it before swallowing it. Then I grit my teeth and resist the urge to grab a stick and knock the holy crap out of him.

Mary Jane reaches over and grabs my hand. We squeeze courage into each other's palms and walk straight ahead like God has parted the Red Sea and the Promised Land is around the next bend.

"Hey, you all want to see what's in my pocket?" Johnny says.

I can practically hear the smirk he must have on his face. Mary Jane gasps. I keep staring at my shoes, like they are the most fascinating worn-out oxfords on earth. Out of the corner of my eye I see Johnny holding the front of his pants.

"You're disgusting!" I yell, before I can stop myself.

Johnny laughs again and Mary Jane and I start running and don't stop until we get to the mailboxes in front of my house. We collapse on the side of the dirt road in a bed of clover gasping for air amidst the dust we rustled up.

"Did you see what he did?" Mary Jane asks, after she's caught her breath. "He's like some old horny dog." She fans her face that is still flushed from running. When Mary Jane runs, her face turns as red as her hair and her freckles blend into the background. "Do you think we should tell somebody?" she adds.

"I don't know," I say. Even though I'm smart when it comes to school subjects, I feel dumb when it comes to Johnny Monroe.

"If I tell Mama and Daddy they may not let me out of the house again until I'm thirty," Mary Jane says. "What about your mama?"

"She'll think I caused it."

"But you didn't."

"I know," I say. "But Mama thinks I draw trouble the way flowers draw bees."

Mary Jane huffs. "Johnny Monroe is as mean as a rattlesnake, and that has nothing to do with you."

Horseflies catch up with us and we swat them again as I ponder what to do about Johnny Monroe. My life would be a lot simpler if he just dropped off the face of the earth. Next time I'm at the cemetery I think I'll ask God to arrange it.

CHAPTER SIX

We rest at the mailboxes at the bottom of our hill.

"Johnny Monroe is like a boil on my backside," I say to Mary Jane, which is about as true a statement as I've ever said. Though I've never had one.

Mary Jane laughs and I catch her laughing like a summer cold. Right there in the middle of the road we double over, tears in our eyes. Laughter is the perfect tonic after being so scared and I wonder if Aunt Sadie should try to bottle our giggles instead of her root concoctions that taste like something you shouldn't put in your mouth.

Cecil Appleby, Meg's ride to work, comes around the corner in his truck a little too fast for the curve. To avoid hitting us, he slams on his brakes, leaving tire tracks in the dirt and a shower of dust behind him. We cough from the dust and laugh more.

My sister, Meg, gets out of the truck and thanks Cecil for the ride. Before he drives away, Cecil gives us a quick lecture on the sheer stupidity of playing in the road. While he does, I can't stop looking at the strawberry birthmark that covers one entire side of his face. Cecil is a deacon at the church and a friend of Preachers.

"Aren't you too old to play in the road?" Meg asks. She sounds a little like Mama. I guess because she's tired.

"We weren't playing in the road," I say. "We were resting and laughing. There's a big difference."

Meg asks Mary Jane about her summer in Arkansas and Mary Jane starts telling about all her J.C. Penney dresses. To avoid temptation, I pick at a scab on my knee until it bleeds. When they quit talking Meg rubs the top of my head, like she used to do when I was younger and I yell at her to stop. She smiles as if pleased that she's irritated me and starts up the hill toward the house. A paperback book sticks out of the top of her purse and I yell that she'd better hide it. She stops long enough to push it deep into her bag and thanks me for looking out for her.

"Maybe we should tell Meg," Mary Jane says. She moves to sit on a big rock next to our mailbox. "She's probably the reason Johnny's hanging around so much anyway."

Tiny grains of grit from the road are in my mouth and I try to spit them out. "If we tell anyone it should be Daniel," I say. "He'll know what to do."

"I like Daniel," she says. "He reminds me of Clark Gable in *Gone with the Wind*."

"Everybody likes Daniel," I say. "And he doesn't look anything like Clark Gable."

Ever since Mary Jane saw the movie in Little Rock, she can't quit talking about it.

We cross the street and climb the hill toward Jo and Daniel's house. In Katy's Ridge everything is on a hill. We find Daniel just home from work and watering his vegetable garden at the back of the house. Late tomatoes and green beans are coming in and a few summer squash. Pumpkins are growing, too. Yellow starburst blooms dot the vines.

"Hey, Wildflower. Hey, Mary Jane," he says when he sees us.

I like that he calls me by my chosen name.

"We need to talk to you," I say, real serious.

He turns over the empty bucket and sits on it like a chair. "I'm ready," he says, a hand on each knee.

Mary Jane passes me a look that says she's just appointed me spokesperson. Words stick in my throat like a primed pump that hasn't pulled water yet. Unlike Mama, who would already be off doing something else, Daniel seems content to wait.

Mary Jane nudges me in the ribs and the words rush out fast. "Johnny Monroe said some things to us he shouldn't have said."

"Like what?" Daniel asks.

My stomach feels jittery, like a hive of bees is buzzing around inside. I can't shake the feeling that God might send lightning or a hailstorm to Katy's Ridge if I tell what Johnny said, and that even though we didn't do anything wrong, I'll end up getting punished for it. I remind myself about what Daddy said about fear being a friend and then wonder if this friend and the secret sense are somehow in cahoots.

"He asked us to go into the woods with him," I say finally, "and he wanted to show us what was in his pocket." The words don't sound as bad as Johnny's actions.

"He unbuttoned his overalls and touched himself!" Mary Jane blurts, like this is the part she's been dying to say.

Daniel's eyes widen, like the whole picture has come as crystal clear as Syler's Pond. He says something under his breath and then rises from his bucket. "I'll take care of it," he says, tucking his shirt-tail into his pants.

"Don't tell Mama," I beg Daniel.

"She's your mama, Wildflower, she has a right to know," he says.

"She'll just ask a bunch of her questions and then blame me for it," I say. "And please don't tell Jo, either."

Daniel chews on a piece of straw like he's thinking hard.

"After Daddy died, you said I could come to you and talk about anything," I remind him. "You said I could trust you." I figure this is just what he needs to be able to keep the secret.

Daniel pauses, like he's giving it some thought. "I guess you don't want your folks to know about it, either," he says to Mary Jane.

"No, sir," she says. "They'll send me to live in Little Rock with my Granny."

Daniel agrees to keep our secret but on the condition that if anything like this happens again, he's telling everybody. Mary Jane and I agree. We even shake on it.

"I'm eating dinner at Mary Jane's," I say, "and we have to walk by Johnny to get back to her house."

"I'll go with you," Daniel offers.

"I have to go tell Mama first, about dinner," I say.

"Come by here when you're ready to go back," Daniel says. "Johnny Monroe won't do anything while I'm around."

For the first time in ages it feels like the boil on my backside might have been lanced. At the house, Mama is busy canning and doesn't catch on that anything has happened. When I tell her I'm eating at Mary Jane's, she looks downright relieved. Before we leave

Mama makes us each a big glass of lemonade and asks Mary Jane about her summer in Little Rock, while stirring a big pot of boiling tomatoes. I can't remember the last time Mama showed this much interest in me. I try not to get jealous because I am sure somewhere in the Bible it says, *Thou shalt not be jealous of thy best friend getting attention,* or some such thing. The Bible has a saying for everything, especially for the things you should not do.

After we drain the last little bit of sugar out of the bottom of our glasses, Mary Jane and I walk to Daniel's house again. We enter the kitchen where Jo is frying okra on the stove and fanning herself with a folded up copy of the Rocky Bluff newspaper.

"I'm going to take a walk with the girls," Daniel says to Jo.

"That's fine," she says, looking radiant even while sweating.

Daniel put his arms around Jo, pats her stomach, and then kisses her on the cheek. Mary Jane smiles as though Fred Astaire and Ginger Rogers have just started dancing in the kitchen. I roll my eyes and hope Mary Jane doesn't come down with the swoons like Meg. Then I'll be the only one left with any sense.

We leave the house with Daniel and when we get to the crossroads, Johnny is nowhere to be seen. For a few seconds I'm disappointed that I won't get to witness a showdown between Daniel and Johnny. It's not like Johnny to have the good sense to leave after saying the things he did.

"Let's pay a visit to his house," Daniel says.

I've never set foot near Johnny's house but Daniel seems to know where it is. We follow the main road another hundred yards and then take a narrow path through the woods littered with trash and broken liquor bottles. Kudzu vines cover the trees making a shroud of shade. We walk deeper and deeper into the woods and I start to remember every fairy tale I've ever read where people get lost in the woods and thrown into ovens or eaten by wolves. When we finally reach the Monroe's house, it isn't even a house, but more like a shack.

As we approach, Daniel calls out, "Is anybody home?"

I can't imagine living anywhere so small and dirty. This house makes ours look like a mansion. A stand of hardwoods surround the shack and make it look even smaller. An oak stands close to the house. One that's young enough that its lower branches can still be climbed. I think of Ruby and imagine the scene I heard Amy and Mama describe in the kitchen a few weeks before. A shudder crawls up my spine.

A crooked porch is attached to the cabin and one of the steps is missing. Wads of yellowed newspaper fill cracks between the boards of the shack. A faded, torn curtain moves from behind the window. Pieces of a face appear: an eye, a cheek. The door opens slowly and catches on a swollen floorboard. The girl peers out.

"Hello, Miss Melody," Daniel says.

"Hello, Mr. Daniel," she says, her words soft. Warily, the girl steps outside, her skin so white it appears to have never seen the sun. Her gaze briefly rests on me and Mary Jane before flitting off like a butterfly lifting from a flower. She brushes a few pieces of stringy hair with her hand, as if her unexpected company warrants a better appearance.

"We're looking for your brother," Daniel says to her.

"Oh," she says. Her eyes shift from left to right and then back to center as if danger could be lurking anywhere.

The look in Melody's eyes reminds me of something I've seen before. The cries of the trapped fox fill my memory, a fox Daddy and I found one time up on the mountain above our house. It was caught in a metal trap. It took forever for Daddy to free it and I covered my ears to try to block out the animal's cries. Finally he covered its head with his flannel coat so it wouldn't bite him and he used his knife to pry the trap open. The fox limped away, its paw nearly severed, leaving a trail of blood behind. Melody's eyes remind me of the fox's eyes.

Rumors around Katy's Ridge have Melody not right in the head. But from what I can tell she'd be perfectly fine if life was gentler with her. I can't imagine what's it like to have a brother like Johnny and I wonder if she misses her sister, Ruby. If I lost one of my sisters, I don't think I would ever recover. I even miss baby Beth, who died when she was two days old, and I never set eyes on her.

Up the hill behind the house, the outhouse door opens with a loud squeak and Johnny steps out. He pulls up his pants and smells his fingers. Just when I thought Johnny Monroe couldn't get more disgusting, he just did. He stops when he sees us, like a crook caught with the goods in his hands. Melody lowers her head and closes the door softly, as if a sleeping baby rests inside.

In the distance, Johnny takes a plug of chewing tobacco from his pocket and sticks it in his mouth. He shuffles toward us and works the chew with his mouth wide open. Then he grabs a tin can lying in a junk pile among pieces of plows and broken tools along with discarded scraps of wood and pieces of rusted animal traps.

Johnny stops when he sees us. The three of us face him, our own version of David facing Goliath. I wish I'd thought to bring the slingshot Daddy made me. I'd aim right for the center of Johnny's forehead and let it rip.

When Johnny gets close enough that we can read the "cling peaches" on his tin can, he stops and spits a big wad of tobacco juice three inches from Daniel's boot. Johnny smiles, as if impressed with his own skill.

Daniel stays calm, with the exception of one fist that he balls up like he's ready to use it.

We stand under the oak tree and I wonder if Ruby is looking down on us. A vibration starts in my chest and I have the secret sense that Ruby wants me to know what happened to her.

"Johnny, I want you to leave these girls alone," Daniel says. His voice carries like he is God speaking from Mt. Sinai.

"I ain't doing nothin' to those girls," Johnny says. He squirts a mouthful of tobacco juice toward the peach can and misses. He snarls, like it is his first miss in years. The lemonade I had earlier turns sour in my stomach. I've spent so much time looking at my shoes, I haven't taken in the full picture of Johnny. His clothes are covered with a month's worth of dirt. His face is dirty, too. And someone must have used a dull kitchen knife to cut his hair because none of it matches up. When the wind kicks up we smell the stink of sour, dirty clothes and days-old sweat.

"I know you, Johnny," Daniel says. "I'm telling you right now, you leave these girls alone or I'll come after you. You hear me?"

Johnny spits again, but this time off to the side.

Daniel narrows his eyes to make good his threat.

"I hear you," Johnny says finally. His smile reveals two missing teeth, tobacco resting in the crevices.

Mary Jane and I follow Daniel down the path. I glance at the oak tree one last time and the vibration in my chest flutters again, as if Ruby is proud of us for standing up to her brother.

"He won't be any more trouble," Daniel says to us. "That boy's all bark and no bite."

I hope Daniel's right. "Why is he so mean?" I ask. Meanness and goodness are a mystery to me. It seems that everybody has a little of both.

Daniel holds back a large sticker bush from the path so Mary Jane and I can pass.

"It's hard to say what makes a person mean," he says. "For one thing, I don't think anybody's cared for that boy a single day of his life."

We step over piles of garbage thrown on the path. A rustle in the underbrush startles us and Mary Jane grabs my hand. Mr. Monroe approaches, cleaning the barrel of his shotgun with a dirty rag.

"Something I can do for you folks?" Mr. Monroe asks. Arthur Monroe makes Johnny look clean cut.

"It's taken care of," Daniel says.

"What's that boy done now?" he asks. He spits in the vines next to him. Spitting must run in this family, like meanness does. Except that Ruby and Melody don't seem mean at all.

"Johnny's been bothering the girls," Daniel says. "But I think we came to an understanding."

"Johnny does have a way with the girls." Old man Monroe grins and scratches a week's worth of whiskers on his dirty face and then looks over at me. "This one's growing up nice, ain't she," he adds. He gives me a wink.

I snap my head in the other direction and try not to gag. Daniel takes my hand and I take Mary Jane's.

"We'll be going now," Daniel says. "Like I said, your boy and I have come to an understanding. I trust there won't be any more trouble."

"Well if there is, you just let me know, and I'll knock the shit out of him," Mr. Monroe says. "That's all that boy understands, anyway."

Mr. Monroe blows his nose on the same dirty rag he used to clean his gun and shoves it into his back pocket. He walks away and staggers against a pine before righting himself.

We go in the opposite direction, moving quickly through the brush. When we reach the road I breathe deep, relieved to be out of the woods and away from Arthur and Johnny Monroe. But something tells me I may never get away from them.

"I feel sorry for that Melody girl," Mary Jane says, her voice just above a whisper.

"She's got it rough," Daniel says. "Maybe she could help Jo out after the baby comes. We can't pay her much, but at least it would get her out of that house."

I like the idea of getting to know Melody better, as long as her brother isn't anywhere around or her father.

"I couldn't believe she wasn't even wearing shoes," Mary Jane says, like there isn't anything more disgraceful. Whenever I see the part of Mary Jane that is like her mother, I try to ignore it, otherwise I might question why we're friends.

"And poor Ruby," Mary Jane continues. "Accidentally killing herself. Have you ever heard of something so awful?"

"She's in a better place," I say, sounding too much like Preacher. But in the back of my mind I'm thinking that what happened to Ruby was no accident.

"Any place would be a better place than that old shack," Mary Jane says.

Mary Jane doesn't even know the part about Ruby going to have a baby and for some reason I feel protective of Ruby's secret.

We reach the crossroads where Mary Jane and I will turn to go to her house.

"I'd better get back. Jo's probably got the okra ready," Daniel says. "You all promise to tell me if there are any more problems?"

"Promise," I say.

"Promise," Mary Jane echoes.

When Mary Jane and I sit down to dinner at her house we don't mention a word about the Monroes.

"Welcome, Louisa May," Mary Jane's father says and then sets out to say the longest prayer in history. I am certain the mashed potatoes will be as cold as buttermilk by the time he finishes and I am right.

We have roast beef, something we eat rarely at my house, but the meat is tough and by the end of supper my jaws hurt from all the chewing. *What a waste*, I think. Mama could have done a much better job with the meal. The mashed potatoes have huge lumps in them and the peas taste scalded. But the plates we eat off of don't have a single chip.

Mary Jane's father has a wooden leg attached at the knee. He took it off and showed it to me once and I studied it for a long time. His knee looked like the nub of an elbow and hung there like a hunk of sausage in the window of Sweeny's store, which Mary Jane's father owns. He lost his leg in a tractor accident when he was eighteen and then gave up farming to open the store in Katy's Ridge. He told me once that his actual severed leg is buried in his mother's back yard in

Arkansas, right next to all their dead pets. For some reason a leg buried among cats, dogs, and rabbits gives me the creeps a lot more than any graveyard.

Mary Jane's brother, Victor, is two years older than me and has all his arms and legs. He works for Mary Jane's father at the grocery store, located on the road to Rocky Bluff. We go there to get bubble gum sometimes and Victor always throws in an extra piece for me. Victor is as close to having a brother as I've ever come. He respects nature, like Daddy taught me, and won't squash a mosquito unless he has to, figuring they have as much right to be alive as any of us.

We used to catch lightning bugs together—me, Mary Jane and Victor—and we'd fill a Mason jar with holes cut in the top. But Victor always made us let them go after we counted them. Tonight, something's different and Victor avoids looking at me in the eyes like he's all of a sudden become shy. He talks to his father about business and keeps looking over like he's trying to impress me with how much he knows about running a store.

Meanwhile, all through supper, Mary Jane's father scratches his wooden leg like it itches. He'd probably unscrew the thing and use it to serve up the cold, lumpy mashed potatoes if he thought it would get a laugh.

Before dark, Meg and Mama show up at Mary Jane's to walk me home. Even though the Sweeney's have everything they could possibly want or need, Mama brings Mary Jane's mother two jars of her canned tomatoes and a small quilt piece she sewed to put hot things on the dinner table.

Our family has a habit of walking in the evenings when the weather is nice. Daddy always said it helped supper digest. But when we walk these days, there's a big hole where Daddy usually stood and I think we all feel it.

No one stands at the crossroads when we walk by. I think of Melody, living in a shack next to the oak tree where her sister Ruby died. I wouldn't wish that life on anybody.

Daddy would say the Monroes deserve our pity. We don't have much, but we are rich compared to them. We are not to judge people who are going through hard times. He was big on being a good person. But people like Johnny make being a good person much harder than it sounds.

The sun has long gone behind the mountain and the moon is rising. Shadows of trees blend with the darkness. Crickets sing their chorus, their music surrounding us.

Meg locks her arm in Mama's. Meg is good at getting Mama's attention in a way that Mama doesn't mind. The moonlight serves as a lantern as we walk in silence, our footsteps shuffling in the dirt. We find our way home in total darkness and it's as if our feet have memorized the path.

Back when Daddy used to walk with us he would hold my hand. I'd be on one side while Mama was on the other. He held Mama's hand a lot, too, like they were still courting. Sometimes he would light his pipe and it would be so dark all we could see was the little bowl of fire kept alive by his breath. He knew the path up the hill to our house better than any of us and he would lead the way, guiding our steps to avoid every rock and root.

Jasmine grows along the path and in summer our noses tell us when we are close to home. I imagine Daddy's footsteps joining ours, him leading the way through the darkness, the smell of sweet tobacco mingling with the smell of jasmine.

About halfway up the hill I shiver, even though it isn't the least bit cold, and wrap my arms around myself. I sense someone watching us in the dark. I immediately think of Johnny and I am about to say something to Meg and Mama when I trip and fall to the ground. A hand jerks me up.

"Don't be clumsy, Louisa May," Mama says. Her grasp pinches my skin and I pull away.

"Are you okay?" Meg asks in the darkness.

"I'm fine," I say. My embarrassment chases away any remaining creepy feelings and I brush the dirt from my hands and knees, missing Daddy more than ever.

CHAPTER SEVEN

The next morning, the screen door slaps at my heels as I walk out on the front porch and a knot twists in my stomach. I have had the secret sense more often the last few days. It starts as a vibration in my chest and then extends to my fingertips like a mild charge of electricity. I pause, remembering a similar feeling the day Daddy died.

"Where you headed, Louisa May?" Mama says from behind me. I jump before I can stop myself.

"Why don't you call me by my real name and maybe I'll tell you," I say. The words come out more hateful than I intend.

"Wildflower..." she says. Her patience is as ragged as Daddy's favorite shirt I keep digging out of the rag bin because she keeps throwing it away.

"I'm not a child, Mama. You don't have to know every single place I go." Although I'm convinced she knows exactly where I'm going and that's the whole point of asking me. She just wants me to say it. It is the anniversary of Daddy's accident and I've been thinking about it all morning. Even if everybody else acts like they've forgotten him, nothing can keep me from going to the graveyard today to pay my respects.

"I'm going to the river," I say, which is a lie. Then I'm down the path before she can stop me.

"Be careful," she yells after me, like she used to say to Daddy every morning he left for the sawmill.

"I will," I yell back, which was always Daddy's answer, too.

Leaves from the poplar trees dot the ground like stars. The poplars are the first to know that fall is coming and the first to drop their leaves. Winter will follow, a hard time in the mountains. Visiting the outhouse with a foot of snow on the ground isn't something anybody looks forward to.

At the crossroads I look out for Johnny, but he isn't around. Daniel's talk must have worked. I take my shortcut, complete with ritual to cross the stream, and minutes later enter the gate in the back of the graveyard. The more I come this way the faster it takes. As I close the gate, my fingers tingle with the electricity of the secret sense. For several seconds I stand without moving, wondering if this means I should turn back.

But it's the anniversary, I say to myself, *Daddy would want me to be with him.* I convince myself to keep going.

When I approach his marker something looks different. The knot in my gut twists tighter, a tingling premonition that something isn't right. Then I see it. A Mason jar, full of clear liquid, lies next to one of the tree roots. The grass is torn up like somebody has stomped around on the grave. I walk closer, feeling like the ground might cave in under me. Daddy's tombstone is streaked with a brown, muddy slash from one end to the other. An empty can is tossed a few feet away on the ground.

I kick the peach can down the hill with all my might. "I hate you, Johnny Monroe!" I yell. A faint echo bounces off a nearby hill.

Tobacco juice spews out in wide, brown arches as the can thumps end over end down the hill toward the river. My anger comes out in tears, which makes me even madder. I yank a handful of willow leaves from the branch closest to me and scrub the stinking tobacco juice off of my father's name. The leaves are too small to do the job so I run up the hill and get poplar and maple leaves which are bigger. After spitting on the leaves, I frantically rub at the brown juice on Daddy's marker. My knuckles get bruised and bloodied against the stone. I can't believe that even Johnny Monroe would do such a vile thing to the memory of a dead person.

Tears blur my vision as I pick up the Mason jar from the ground and open it. A repulsive stink spreads, worse than any skunk. Moonshine. The same stuff some of the men from the mill passed around behind the church, after Jo and Daniel's wedding. My face grows hot as I imagine Johnny Monroe spitting tobacco juice on Daddy's grave. Careful not to touch where Johnny Monroe's mouth has been, I throw the jar into the woods.

Revenge fills my mind. Revenge I can't act on. Daniel must have made Johnny really mad and he wants me to know it. Telling Daniel again might make Johnny do something even worse, like come after me or Meg or one of my family. If he's willing to defile the final resting place of a good man who was kind to him, I know now that there is nothing so low that Johnny Monroe wouldn't do.

Since it's the anniversary of when everything in my life changed, my tender memories feel all exposed.

"I'm sorry, Daddy," I say. "It's all my fault."

I wrap my arms around his marker, touching my cheek to the rough stone. It smells of crushed leaves mixed with tobacco and it feels cool to my touch, even in the noonday sun. The coolness reminds me of the day he died. His skin kept getting cooler as the warmth left him, like a fire slowly dying away. I force the memory away, wanting only to remember the good things.

In the distance, Miss Mildred practices the organ for Sunday service, the faint tune resembling *The Old Rugged Cross*. Johnny Monroe knows better than to get anywhere near the church on Sundays, on account of Preacher wanting to snatch his soul from the devil and claim it for the Lord. Preacher would probably get an extra reward in heaven for bagging a big sinner like Johnny. To hear Preacher talk, saving souls is like a baseball game between God and the Devil. Every sinner saved is a home run for the Lord. But Johnny deserves to suffer the fires of hell. If I wasn't convinced of this before, I am now.

The willow tree sways with the breeze and the sun flickers from behind the clouds. A small whirlwind dances on Daddy's grave before skirting down the hillside toward the mound of newly packed earth on top of Ruby Monroe. Her grave remains unmarked, except that somebody has placed a handful of wilted flowers on top of the dirt. Ruby will probably never have a marker because the Monroe's are too poor to get one and it isn't like anybody at the church will take up a collection for it, either, like they did for Daddy.

A twig snaps behind me and I jump. Fear crackles up my spine. Word is there are still mountain lions up in the high hills, though nobody have seen one for over twenty years.

"Well, look who's here," a voice says. In that instant I know that it's a human predator I am dealing with instead of an animal one.

The shock of seeing Johnny Monroe freezes me in my tracks. Goosebumps crawl up my arms. His clothes are covered with dirt and he has a bruise under one eye like somebody beat the fire out of him.

"Hello, Johnny," I say, hiding my fear. If you come across a rattlesnake you're supposed to stop, then slowly back away. But I am still on my knees and backing away isn't an option.

"I thought I'd come visit your daddy," he grins. Whoever blackened his eye, knocked out one of his teeth, too. "Yeah, me and your daddy had a little party up here last night. Did you know he liked moonshine whiskey?"

I clinch my jaw. Anger surges inside me again, but I figure this is just what Johnny wants, an excuse to come after me. I force myself to take a deep breath instead of the short, jagged ones my anger insists on.

"What's wrong? Cat got your tongue?" He pokes me in the shoulder.

"No, I just need to be going, that's all," I say. "Mama's waiting for me."

"No she's not," he says. "I bet she has no idea you're up here."

My insides churn. Johnny is right. He moves closer. His breath stinks of moonshine.

I start to stand, but Johnny pushes me back down. "You ain't goin' no place," he says. He grabs my wrist and squeezes tight. It hurts like blue blazes. When I try to pull away, he holds me fast.

"Okay, maybe I can stay for a while," I say. Even though I act calm, my heart is racing. I decide my best chance of getting out of there is to act like Johnny's friend. "How are you and your Daddy doing, Johnny? I was so sorry about Ruby."

He looks confused and glances over his shoulder at Ruby's grave. For a split second I wonder if he put those flowers there himself. Maybe he misses her. But when he looks back at me I know his rage has left no room for tender heartedness. I wonder if I can outrun him. Maybe if I catch him by surprise. His eyes narrow, as if he has heard my thoughts.

"You don't care about my family," he says.

"It must be hard not having a mother," I say. "Kind of like me not having a father."

I've never seen Johnny Monroe look puzzled. "I've been watching you," he says through gritted teeth.

"So what," I say, trying to act casual. "People watch other people all the time."

Johnny holds my wrist tighter. In the distance, Miss Mildred and Preacher come out of the church. I yell to them, "Hey, up here! Help!"

Johnny puts his hand over my mouth and squeezes my face. His grip hurts and his hands smell of tobacco. When I scream again, it comes out muffled. Besides, Preacher and Miss Mildred are far enough away that it won't do any good. Preacher locks the door even though there's nothing in there worth stealing—a few hymnals is all, and Miss Mildred's organ, which I can't imagine anyone taking the time to lug down the road.

After they leave, Johnny uncovers my mouth and grabs my wrist again. He looks smug, like he's gotten away with something.

"I really need to go, Johnny. Daniel's going to come looking for me any minute." When I try to jerk free, his grip tightens until my fingers turn white.

"Daniel don't know you're up here. Nobody does. I saw you leave your house," Johnny says.

I knew he'd been watching me and this just confirms it. "Let's just forget all this," I say. "I'll go home and you can get on back to standing on your road and nobody has to know anything about it. I'll even put in a good word about you to Meg."

Johnny leans closer and runs his free hand up and down my arm like he is calming a calf before slitting its throat.

A breeze blows through the willow tree and jiggles the leaves like gold coins. Johnny touches my hair. His hand is awkward, clumsy. "You like that, don't you," he says. His try at tenderness is scarier than his roughness.

I pull away, but the vice of his grip holds firm.

"You're feisty, aren't you?" Johnny says. "I like feisty."

The voice in my head screams out for help, but I am alone. Daddy is gone. I fight back the sadness as hard as I fight back Johnny. It doesn't matter how loud or how long I scream up here, nobody will hear me.

"Johnny you need to let me go," I say again, my voice sweet as molasses. "Your mama wouldn't like you acting like this."

"My mama didn't give a shit about me," he says. He spits and I see in his eyes how much he believes it.

"I'm sure she would be here to help you out if she could, Johnny. Just like my daddy would be here to help me out if he could."

"Your daddy can't do nothin' for you now," he says, "not since he got hisself cut in half."

Johnny's words grip my chest like he's reached in and squeezed my heart with his dirty, bare hands. I aim my fist right at Johnny's nose and swing and hit him as hard as I can. The punch connects. He moans. Blood squirts from his nose onto my face.

"You bitch!" he yells. He grabs his nose and loosens his grip long enough for me to pull away. I run for the shortcut as fast as my legs will go, forcing myself to not look back or it will slow me down. My feet pound the ground with every step, yet it feels like I've sprouted wings. I leap over roots and branches and anything in the path. I've never run this hard. I smile with the thought that I might get away. Then I hear Johnny coming down the hill behind me.

My heart pumps wildly. The footbridge lies over the next rise. If I can make it to the bridge and get across before him, I might have a chance. Johnny weighs more than me. He'll have to slow down to get across. I grip the necklace around my neck while I run and ask Daddy and God and Mary to save me, and anybody else in heaven that will listen.

Through the trees I catch sight of the old footbridge up ahead. Johnny's breathing is heavy and close. Just when I think I'm going to make it, he tackles me to the ground. The fall knocks the breath out of me. I gasp for air. Johnny flips me over hard. He yanks my hair. His nose is red and swollen. Blood streaks across his face like cat's whiskers. His stink smothers me, a foul stench of moonshine, tobacco and rotten teeth. He pins my shoulders to the ground.

At that moment the thought occurs to me that the two things I fear most are right in front of me: Johnny Monroe and the threat of dying young. If Johnny has his way, he'll put me in the grave right next to Daddy so he can spit tobacco juice on my name, too.

Out of breath, Johnny leans over me and smothers me with his body. His whiskers hurt, brushing my cheeks and neck like a thousand sharp needles. He yanks my hands over my head and holds them there. I pull hard against his grasp but have no strength to move him. Johnny forces his mouth against mine and I taste his rotten spit. I gag and choke. Then he bites my lip and shoves his tongue down my throat. I struggle, jerking my mouth free.

"Johnny, don't!" I cry. He grins at me and I feel like I am looking into the face of the devil himself.

"There's nobody here that can save you," Johnny says, and I believe him.

Then he slaps me so hard my ears ring like the treble notes of Miss Mildred's organ. I taste blood in my mouth and my face is hot and stinging with pain. I turn my head to the side and throw up. This seems to make him even angrier. He slaps me again. The pain is a hundred times worse than anything I've ever felt. When I scream again he covers my mouth with his hand. I bite his hand hard and he slaps me, closed fisted again, so hard this time the pain crescendos into numbness. Urine soaks my underwear and the warmth spreads down my legs.

Seconds later, the pain goes away. I have the odd feeling that I am floating outside of myself, watching the scene. This isn't happening to me at all, but to a stranger, some other foolish thirteen-year-old girl who didn't listen to her secret sense and is powerless to get away.

"What's the matter, Louisa May?"

"My name's Wildflower," I mumble, defiant.

"Wildflower?" he laughs, "Nah . . . people should call you Weed." He grabs my hair again and pulls. "Yeah, I think I'll pull this weed."

As he drags me screaming to a clearing, I search the woods for salvation. But the chance of anyone finding me is about as slim as the chance that Johnny will have a change of heart. Hot tears streak my face and pool in my ears. I tell them to stop so Johnny won't see my weakness but they keep on like the trickle of a stream seeking the river.

"Let's get you comfortable," he says, pulling me over on a bed of leaves. It's as if his motions have nothing to do with me. I could be anybody, or anything—an animal he wrestled to the ground. He pulls a jack knife from his pocket and unfolds it. Then he waves it in front of me, inches from my face. The metal glitters in the patchy sun, as if recently sharpened.

Something moves in the distance and I look past him into the trees. I gasp. Ruby Monroe is hanging by the neck swinging in the breeze. Her eyes, wide open, stare down at me. I watch her until the image fades away.

"What are you looking at?" Johnny says. He throws down his knife, takes my jaw in his hands and holds my head so that I have to look at him.

"Nothing," I say, as if I might get Ruby in trouble.

He rips off my dress; the new one Amy made me for my birth- day that I put on this morning in honor of the anniversary of Daddy's death. The seams are tight and not easily torn, but he man- ages with the help of his knife. The air is cool on my skin. He stares at the yellowing camisole that all my sisters wore before me. Then he takes his knife and cuts it off. His eyes take in my fledgling breasts and he cups a rough hand over each. I dig my heels in the dirt and push away. He pulls me back.

"Well, look at this," he says. He holds Grandma McAllister's medallion in his hand. "Looks like real gold."

"Leave that alone," I say through clenched teeth. He rips the necklace from my neck. The chain stings my skin and I remember what Jesus said in the Bible about not throwing your pearls before swine. But Jesus didn't say what to do if the swine turned out to be bigger than you and stole your pearls without asking.

Johnny gazes at the necklace. For a moment, his eyes soften. But then he sees me watching him and his expression changes as fast as a lightning strike. He touches his nose. A fresh trickle of blood comes from inside. With new determination, he wraps his fingers around my neck until I can't breathe. I squirm to get away and search his face for a sign of mercy. There is none. It occurs to me that Johnny Monroe's hateful face will be the last thing I see before I die.

He loosens his grip to whisper in my ear, and I suck much-needed air into my lungs. "If you tell anybody about this, I'll kill you," he says. "Y'hear that? You can't hide from me. I'll find you and kill you dead!"

I nod, thinking it's over, that Johnny's had a change of heart. He's going to let me go, as long as I promise not to ever tell anyone. But instead he tightens his grip again and unhooks the belt on his pants. There is no fight left in me. My heartbeat echoes in my ears. I pray to God to be rescued and ask him to send Daddy. I offer wordless prayers to the trees, the river, and the land and then apologize to Mama for getting myself hurt and to Aunt Sadie for not paying attention to what she taught me about the secret sense.

I close my eyes and surrender. Seconds later Daddy comes toward me. He stands, surrounded by light, and holds out his hand for me to take. I float toward the treetops to meet him and he takes me into his arms. When I look back, I see my body still lying on the ground, Johnny on top of me. I wonder briefly how I can be two places at once. But it doesn't really matter. All that matters is that Daddy is here. A year ago he left, but now he's back. He's come to take me with him.

CHAPTER EIGHT

One Year Earlier

Daniel McBride comes to the schoolhouse during recess. I've seen him around because he works at the Blackstone sawmill with Daddy. Jo has had a secret crush on him ever since he came to our house last Christmas. Daddy always invites anybody that doesn't have family nearby to come to our house on holidays because he says we have enough family and food to share. Daniel used to live up North and he is the only Yankee I've ever seen up close. Since jobs were scarce, he moved to Rocky Bluff to take a position with the railroad. When that didn't work out he took a job at the sawmill, where Daddy is his supervisor. Most people have forgiven him for being a Yankee on account of how nice he is.

Breathless, Daniel's sweat soaks into his shirt. He leans over and whispers something to Mr. Webster, my teacher since first grade, who is sitting in the shade grading papers. Mr. Webster turns and looks over at me on the swing, his face solemn. Mr. Webster is strict, but fair, and always wears a suit coat like being a school teacher is as important as the President of the United States.

"Louisa May, you need to go home right away," Mr. Webster says.

"Why?" I ask. I've never in six years of schooling been told to go home.

He looks at Daniel and then back at me. "You're needed at home," he repeats, as if this is all the reason I should need.

"But why?" I ask. "What's happened?"

Mr. Webster hardens his face and I remember the last time I had to write *I will not talk back to Mr. Webster* a hundred times on the blackboard.

"Come on, Louisa May," Daniel says. He stands and motions toward the truck.

"What's going on?" Mary Jane asks, walking over from the swing.

"Nobody will say," I tell Mary Jane, "but it can't be good."

"Good luck," Mr. Webster says as I leave.

It feels weird for Mr. Webster to wish me anything, especially good luck. Not to mention how strange it is to go home so early in the day. Sometimes on the last day of school we get to go home early, but never at the first of the year and never before lunch. Even if a big snowstorm hits, we are expected to make it in and stay the full day.

Daniel holds the door open to the sawmill truck while I step inside. He gets in on the drivers side and starts the truck. Flecks of sawdust stick to the sweat on his forehead.

"What's happened?" I ask, still trying to get answers.

He hesitates, as if weighing the consequences of his words, and then says, "There's been an accident. They're taking your daddy home."

"If he's had an accident, why aren't they taking him to the hospital in Rocky Bluff?" I ask.

Daniel pauses again, his arms resting on the steering wheel. When he finally speaks his voice is softer than I expect. "We'll find out when we get you home."

My chest tightens, making it harder to breathe. Something is up, and I am convinced that *something* isn't good. "Does Mama know?" I ask.

"Yes. She's waiting at the house," he says.

We ride in silence the whole way and it is the longest ride home I've ever had. I am afraid to ask any more questions, afraid to know the truth, or maybe I don't want to make Daniel more uncomfortable than he already is. Though he seems nice enough, I hardly know him at all.

Daniel takes it slow over the bluff like everyone does, respecting the sheer drop that accompanies any false turn. After the road levels off, he parks below our house, securing the parking brake despite the level ground. I jump out of the truck and run ahead, realizing halfway up the hill that I forgot to thank him for the ride.

When I get to the house Meg is sitting on the porch sniffing back a steady stream of tears. Her face is red and puffy like it always gets whenever she cries. She stayed home from school to help Mama with some canning. Otherwise she'd be at the high school.

"What happened, Meg?" I ask. Her sobbing commences and I know I won't be getting any answers from her.

Crying is the last thing I feel like doing. I want to know what happened. It doesn't make sense for Daddy to get into an accident at work. It isn't like him to be careless. Once when I went over there he showed me all the machinery and blades not to get close to. If he did get hurt I am certain it can be fixed.

I find Mama in the house sitting at the kitchen table, her face as pale as the bag of White Lily flour on the counter. Daniel comes in behind me and she thanks him for getting me.

"Where's Daddy?" I ask her.

"They're bringing him from the mill," she tells me. Then she looks at Daniel, "Why can't I just go there?" she asks.

"It's best you don't," he says. "They'll bring him by truck until they reach the bottom of the hill."

Daniel puts a hand on Mama's shoulder and I wait for her to slap it away, but she just lets it sit there. In all my twelve years of life, I've never once seen Mama follow orders or sit still. I know at that moment that something is horribly wrong.

"Shouldn't he be here by now?" she asks Daniel.

"Any minute," he answers.

She wrings her hands like they are one of her old mops. Then she gets up and walks through the house to the front porch. We follow. Her eyes are trained down the hill toward the road, watching for Daddy to come home. Sometimes in the evenings she'll watch for him, too, but with a different look on her face, like a schoolgirl waiting for a glimpse of her beau.

We wait, all of us looking down the hill, and I sit on the bottom porch step and kick at dirt clods with my shoe. A fly lights on my knee and walks around, tickling my leg. I catch it in my open fist and let it buzz against the inside of my palm before I set it free. At that moment I feel like that fly. Trapped, and waiting for something bigger to set me free.

We hear them before we see them. A scraping sound first, and then voices growing in volume as they approach. Men are talking to Daddy, encouraging him to hold on.

As they turn the corner we see an old mule pulling a wooden stretcher up the hill. It isn't really a stretcher but something that farmers use to pull firewood or move harvested crops from one end of a field to another. I've never seen it used to pull a person and wonder who came up with the idea. Daddy is wrapped up in blankets like it's the dead of winter, even though it is a warm day in October. Indian Summer, it's called. I don't know why. Next time I see Horatio Sector I'll have to ask. If anybody knows, he will. The Indians have lived in these mountains longer than anybody.

Nailed to where I stand, I wait for Daddy to lift his head and catch my eye and smile at me to let me know everything is okay. But the bundle that is supposed to be my father doesn't move.

The mule labors up the path, with the stretcher scraping the ground behind it. I've never heard that sound before—wood scraping against rock and dirt—and it strikes me that the men should be carrying him instead of dragging. The hill never seemed that steep to me before. I've run up and down it from the time I was knee high. But the mule struggles with Daddy's weight and one of the men slaps its backside to keep it moving. The men and the stretcher look like they are coming up the hill in slow motion.

Meg cries harder the closer they get and the redness of her face has turned to splotches. Daniel holds onto her while Mama runs down the hill to meet the men. I've never seen Mama run like that. She has a quickness about her like someone younger. She calls

Daddy's name and the men part to let her join them. Daddy lies in the center like a king coming to a palace, except it is our house he is being taken to and there aren't any servants except these men from the mill.

I break from my trance and run down the path to meet him, too, but one of the men grabs me before I get too close.

"Easy there," he says. "Your daddy's hurt real bad."

I jerk my shoulder away. When I look down I see a piece of burlap wrapping Daddy soaked dark red. Blood. It is odd to see him lying there not moving. I don't understand how a man that towers over most people can look so small on a stretcher. As far as I'm concerned, Jesus learned how to walk on water from him so it makes no sense that he might be drowning in his own blood. I'm not sure the stain on the cloth is his blood anyway. Somebody could have just put it there. It occurs to me that maybe this is a joke Daddy is playing on us and any minute he'll hop up and laugh his hearty laugh that he's pulled a prank and we fell for it.

"Daddy, open your eyes. Look at me," I say. "It's Wildflower."

I wish so hard that he open his eyes that he actually does. But he opens them like they weigh a ton.

"Daddy, what's wrong?" I say.

He turns to look at me, and I see in his eyes more than I want to. He is hurt bad. In an instant his look tells me how sorry he is that he won't get to see me grow up. This truth makes my knees buckle underneath me and one of the men catches me right as I am falling and holds onto me until I can stand upright again. This is the closest I've ever come to fainting and it takes me several steps to get the ground solid underneath me again.

"It's okay, Daddy," I say, walking alongside him up the hill. His eyes open and close every few seconds like he is the sleepiest he has ever been. I want to be strong so he won't feel so bad, and it looks like Mama is doing the same. She holds onto his hand as they make the rest of the way up the hill.

"I love you, Joseph," she keeps saying, strong and solid. "Now, don't you go leaving me. You're the best thing that's ever happened to me."

I feel like I am hearing things I shouldn't be hearing—things that Mama and Daddy don't say in front of anybody else. I am embarrassed that all of Daddy's men heard it, too. To hide my embarrassment, I watch the mule's tail swish back and forth as it hauls the stretcher up the hill. I recognize the mule to be Simon Hatcher's, a man who owns a farm over near the mill.

When the mule stops in front of the porch, Mama says to the men, "Let's get him to the bed."

The four men carefully lift Daddy and carry him up the front porch steps and into their bedroom. He looks the color of the ashes in the wood stove.

Mama leaves to go into the kitchen and comes back with a cloth to wipe Daddy's face. If one of us kids gets sick she always wipes our foreheads with a cold cloth.

Just about the time the men get Daddy situated on the bed, Doc Lester shows up. Every time I see Doc Lester I think of weasels because of the shape of his face. His chin juts out to a point; plus his eyes are beady and too close together. The men step back into the corners of the room, leaving Mama standing at the head of the bed next to Daddy.

Doc Lester places his small black bag on the foot of the bed and peels back the layers of what Daddy is wrapped in. He blocks my view and the only thing I can see is Doc Lester's weasel-like head shake back and forth.

"Poor devil," he mutters. "He's lost a lot of blood." His voice sounds about as grim as a person can sound.

Somebody nudges me on the shoulder and it is Daniel McBride. "Why don't we go outside?" he says, looking out toward the porch.

"But I want to see," I say.

"Best to leave this to the grown-ups," Daniel says. He takes me gently by the arm and leads me toward the front door.

"But I just turned twelve," I say, as if this constitutes being grown up. But I let him lead me out of the room anyway.

As I leave the house, I hear Mama gasp when she sees what is underneath the wrappings. An uneasy feeling settles into the pit of my stomach.

A dazed Meg sits on the porch, her face streaked with tears and crimson, as if the color lost in Mama and Daddy faces has become hers.

"Oh my God, Louisa May, we've lost Daddy!" Meg says. Her voice cracks under the weight of the words. I don't like that she's given up on him so easily.

"Where's Jo and Amy?" I ask.

"When Mama got word they were bringing Daddy home, she sent Jo to pick up Amy at the high school."

"I need to go back," I say to Daniel. "He would want me there." I jerk away from Daniel's grip.

Inside, Doc Lester covers Daddy up and closes his little black bag. "Somebody get Preacher. I've done all I can do here."

"He's on his way," a voice says from the back.

Doc Lester is the only doctor in Katy's Ridge, although it is a stretch of the imagination to call him that. He is also the person who signs the death certificates. Preacher being there is merely a courtesy. I push Doc Lester aside and take my place next to Daddy. His eyes are closed and his mouth, stretched tight in pain, is absent the smile he usually wears.

"Hey, Daddy. It's Louisa May."

He doesn't say anything back. Mama sits on the bed putting a cool rag on his head and I wonder if she realizes that he has more than a fever. Next she'll be breaking out the castor oil and the wooden spoon.

"Daddy?" I whisper, leaning next to him. "It's Wildflower."

"Don't bother him, honey," Mama says, as if I'm trying to ask him a question while he's reading. My face burns. I want to shake some sense into her. Does she not see what is happening?

Daddy's eyes open. They used to be as brown as rich shoe leather, but now are black and dull.

"What happened, Daddy?" I ask.

He looks up at me like he has a lifetime of things to tell me. I know he loves me. But what I see in his eyes is more than love. He is telling me that he will miss me. A lump of sorrow lodges in my throat. I swallow so I won't cry.

"Take care of your mama," he says, his beautiful baritone voice now raspy.

This isn't what I want to hear. I want him to tell me that everything is going to be all right, and that he'll be better soon. Instead, he is letting me know that nothing is ever going to be all right again.

"Promise me," he says.

"I will," I say, not even knowing what I'm promising to do. As far as I'm concerned, it is Mama's job to take care of me, not the other way around. But I will agree to anything at that moment if it will take that look from his eyes. I silently beg God to make him better and promise all sorts of things in return. If God wants me to, I will even stop thinking that Preacher and Doc Lester are idiots every time I see them.

Daddy turns his eyes toward Mama. She strokes his cheek with such tenderness I can't bear to watch. I look out the window at a squirrel burying an acorn under the pine tree and wonder how squirrels remember where they've buried things. Do they make little treasure maps in the tops of trees? When I turn back, Daddy's eyes are closed forever.

Dying seems like such a private thing, even with a dozen people in the room. I want to shield him from the watchers, but it is too late. Doc Lester picks up Daddy's wrist searching for a pulse.

"He's gone," he says, opening his silver pocket watch to note the time.

"Gone where?" I ask.

Doc Lester ignores my question and puts an arm on Mama's shoulder. Mama stares down at Daddy, her eyes vacant, like she's gone, too.

"Somebody tell me what's going on," I say too loud.

Nobody answers. Daddy is the one who always answers my questions, and in the next instant, I realize that I will miss this fiercely. At the same time I keep expecting him to open his eyes and smile and ask, "How's my Wildflower?" Then he'll sit up and say he feels much better now and I'll tell him how he gave us all quite a scare.

Miracles have been known to happen in Katy's Ridge. Little Wiley Johnson almost drowned last summer. Everybody was crying over him, too, when all of a sudden he spit out a gallon of the lake and choked air back into his lungs. His parents gave Preacher a big offering the next Sunday on account of God giving back their little boy. Afterwards, Preacher said Wiley was destined to do Jesus' work and spread his gospel. Wiley didn't look too thrilled about that. I don't think he has anything against Jesus, but he is still just a kid.

Seconds later, Aunt Sadie arrives breathless at the door. The men part to let her pass. The noise she makes when she sees Daddy is the most lonesome wail I've ever heard and it sends ripples through me because it is the sound my heart is making, too.

"Everybody out!" Sadie says, and all the men from the mill obey, until there is just me and Sadie and Mama in the room.

"What's happening, Aunt Sadie? What's going on?" I whisper, like my regular voice might wake Daddy up.

"The world just became a much sadder place," Sadie says.

I step closer and touch Daddy's fingers and wait for them to close around mine and for his lungs to fill deep and wide like whenever he takes in a big breath of fresh mountain air first thing in the mornings.

"Breathe, Daddy," I whisper, praying for a Wiley Johnson sized miracle. I take a big breath myself to show him how it's done.

"It won't do any good, sweetheart," Aunt Sadie says. "It's too late."

I hear the words but refuse to believe them. I tell Mama that Aunt Sadie is wrong. But Mama won't stop staring at Daddy. It's as if somebody yelled "freeze" and she got stuck like a statue.

Just then I remember the little package I received when my grandmother McAllister died. Inside was a small, gold medallion of Jesus as a baby in his mother's lap. People all over the world and especially in Ireland, where our people are from, believe that Mary can grant miracles and they pray to her all the time.

I run into my bedroom and take the medallion out of my dresser drawer. It is still in the box, wrapped in white tissue paper, along with a card with a prayer written on it. I read the words on the card and repeat them over and over again, trying to pray up a miracle. At our church in Katy's Ridge, Jesus' mother isn't talked about much. The only time Preacher mentions her is on Christmas day when we hear the story about her giving birth to Jesus in a stable when there was no room at the inn.

I pray so hard that Mary's face is imprinted on my hand. In the meantime, I wait for the miracle. I bite my bottom lip hard enough that it starts to bleed and taste the salty sweetness of my own blood. As far as I can tell, Mama doesn't even realize I am there. She just keeps rubbing Daddy's forehead with the cool rag. It makes me angry, how useless she is. But I am useless, too. Death makes everybody useless. The pain in my lip takes my mind away from the pain that starts to creep in around my heart. I go outside to continue my praying there.

A bunch of men from the mill stand under the pine trees, smoking cigarettes, with their heads bowed and voices low. Daniel sits on the top step of the porch and I go to sit next to him, still clutching the medallion.

"I'm sorry," Daniel says softly.

"Sorry for what?" I ask. "You didn't do anything."

"I'm sorry that your daddy's passed on," Daniel says.

"Passed on to what?" I ask, genuinely curious what he means. "Is he in heaven now? Just like that? One minute you're here and the next minute you're sitting around with angels?"

Daniel looks over at me like he isn't sure how to answer.

"Well, if anybody gets to sit with the angels, it would be your father," he says.

"But what if there's been a mistake and it isn't his time yet? Does God take it back?" The questions whirl around in my mind so fast they make me feel dizzy.

"I don't think there's been a mistake," Daniel says. "I think it was just a horrible accident."

Seconds later, Jo and Amy run up the hill. "What's happened?" Jo asks, out of breath. The men under the pines are a chorus of muteness.

Daniel stands as if he is going to break the news to her but I blurt it out before he has a chance.

"Daddy's had a horrible accident, Jo. He's dead."

Jo and Amy look at me like I've just said the worst stream of bad words imaginable. Jo doesn't believe me at first and asks Daniel what I am talking about.

"It's true," he says. "I'm so sorry."

Amy's eyes are like full moons. She isn't the type to cry but tears fill her eyes and spill over onto her cheeks. Jo and Amy collapse into each others' arms and then Meg joins them from the porch and then I follow and it is the four of us sisters holding onto each other for dear life like we've just been thrown into a lifeboat together on the Titanic.

Things like this aren't supposed to happen to my family. Daddy is supposed to live to be a hundred, setting a record for Katy's Ridge.

Outdoing Cecil Ludlow by one year, who died in his sleep at ninety-nine, after having just rocked one of his great-great granddaughters.

Later that afternoon, Mama breaks from her trance and lays Daddy's hand down like it is a robin's egg she is returning to a nest. Then she goes into the kitchen, puts on her apron and gets busy. From the empty look in her eyes, I know that I have lost Mama, too. In a matter of hours it feels like I have gone from having two, full-fledged parents to being an orphan.

I run out the front door, jumping from the porch to the ground without touching a step like I used to when I was younger. Then I run down the hill, not knowing where I am going, I just have to run. If I don't I might suffocate from the sadness that threatens to drown me.

I jump over deep ruts made by the stretcher and reach the dirt road at the bottom of the hill in no time at all. Still running, I turn onto the river road. My shoes rub at my heels and I stop my flight long enough to toss them into the bushes. Mama will have a fit if she finds out, but I don't care. I run barefoot toward the river. With each stride I try to forget seeing Daddy being pulled up the hill by Simon Hatcher's mule and all the men he worked with. The same men who visited our house last Christmas and who today carried him so carefully from the stretcher to the bed.

As I run I try to make sense of what has happened, but it is like a horrible dream that I don't know how to wake up from. I want the day to start over. I want my father to be standing in the kitchen filling his thermos and kissing my mother before he goes to work. I want him to come home safe and sound like he always does.

Only old people are supposed to die, and sometimes babies if they are sick. Nobody is supposed to die who is strong and healthy and happy. It goes against the nature of things. A person dying young makes life seem unfair and too scary. It means it could happen to any of us, at any time, when we least expect it.

At the end of the road, I stop and rest my hands on my knees to catch my breath. I haven't run like that since the end of the year races in seventh grade. I came close to winning that year and if Freddie Myers had skipped school that day, like he did most days once planting season commenced, I would have won the ribbon.

The look of the land changes the closer I get to the river, as if the mountains are intent on flattening out to greet it. Making my way through tall grass, I follow the path that Daddy and I must have walked together a thousand times. I smell the water before I see it and emerge from the grasses at a small sandy beach. The sight of the water causes me to sigh. Visiting the riverbank is like visiting an old friend. I collapse on a mound of earth, still refusing to cry. Crying might make it too real.

I take in a few deep breaths. Then like a summer rain that sneaks up on a sunny day, the tears come. They arrive slowly at first and I wipe each one away as it falls. But pretty soon I am caught in a downpour of tears, at the very place Daddy and I have fished since the time the grasses were taller than me.

When I got older he showed me how to clean the trout we caught, and one Christmas gave me a special knife to use. I never liked cleaning fish, but Daddy was proud that I was more like him instead of my sisters. They scream at the sight of any kind of fish guts, like I'd torn out my very own eyeball for them to see.

Memories flood over me, and then I remember the last time we were together, earlier that morning.

"*Have a good day at school,*" *Daddy says, giving me a kiss on the forehead. He's kissed me in that same spot so many times I half expect there to be a worn-out place where his lips touch, like the worn-out place on the kitchen rug where Mama always stands to cook.*

"*School is so boring,*" *I say, rolling my eyes.*

"*There's too much to discover for life to be boring,*" *Daddy says back to me.* "*Study the birds, the trees, the patterns on leaves. There's always something new to see.*"

It is just like him to say something special like that.

"*Waiting on your sister again?*" *he asks, buttoning the top button of his work shirt.*

I nod. Meg always makes us late to school with her prissing.

I hold my stomach and feel a little sick. Not sick-sick, but like a bad storm is coming. "*Are you okay?*" *Daddy asks.*

"*I guess,*" *I say.* "*I just feel a little funny.*"

He feels my forehead where he kissed to see if I have a fever.

"*Daddy, don't treat me like I'm a little girl,*" *I say.*

He smiles. "*Forgive me, honey, but you'll always be my little girl,*" *he says.*

I lean into him, knowing I don't really need to forgive him for anything.

"*Do you believe in the secret sense?*" *I ask him.* "*Aunt Sadie told me about it yesterday.*"

"*Our grandmother had it,*" *he says.* "*She could always tell when someone in our village was about to pass on or she would know just when somebody needed something. A kind word. A cup of tea.*"

"*Sadie says I have the gift, too,*" *I say.*

"*Then you probably do,*" *he says. He smiles like he's just found another reason to be proud of me.*

"*You two are like two peas in a pod,*" *Mama says from behind the screen door. She startles me, with her way of showing up all unexpected.*

"Gotta go to work," he says, winking at me.

"Be careful, Joseph," Mama says.

"You know I will," he says. He throws Mama a kiss and smiles. Mama calls Daddy's smile the "famous McAllister smile." In an old photograph of my grandfather you can see the same smile. Whenever I have private time in front of the mirror in the kitchen, which isn't that often given my three older sisters, I practice that smile. I want to be the first girl in our family to have it.

Daddy grabs his thermos and lunch pail off the top step and starts down the hill. "Take care of that stomach of yours," he says to me.

I'd almost forgotten the feeling in the pit of my stomach and now wonder if this could have anything to do with the secret sense.

He throws up his hand in a goodbye, but doesn't look back. About halfway down the path he begins to whistle like he does every day on his way to work. His whistling often takes over where his banjo can't go. I watch him until he is totally out of sight, with the strange feeling that I might never see him again.

Sitting beside the deep flowing river, I try to imagine a life where Daddy never whistles or plays the banjo again. A whole new shower of tears begins, and I am glad I am alone with only the river watching me. After a while, I am so worn out with sadness I fall asleep and don't wake up until after the sun has gone behind the ridge. The breeze on the water is cool now and I wish I'd thought to bring a sweater. A maple tree showers down crispy leaves that have started to change colors. The tips of the green leaves are edged in yellow and red. Daddy taught me about trees. He believes that trees are angels, and that a person can pray to trees or the river or the land just like a person can pray to God. We only cut down trees if we absolutely have to, and even then we make sure we make good use of them and thank them for their service. I never thought about how hard that might have made his job at the sawmill. Seeing all those trees come down.

A fish breaks the surface a few feet away, breaking the spell of my memories. I push away the thought that Daddy and I will never stand on this bank together again. After I wipe the last of my tears, I get up to walk back home. Now we are the family with a house of mourning.

I shiver and wrap my arms around myself. The leaves of the maple burn red with the setting sun like the burning bush appearing to Moses. I take this as a sign that on this day my whole life has changed forever.

CHAPTER NINE

A crowd has gathered back at the house. Every light is on and every window open. Neighbors sit on the porch drinking coffee and smoking their hand-rolled cigarettes. It is like a giant party, but nobody is smiling and their voices are low and muffled. Max, Aunt Sadie's dog, is taking a nap and blocks the door into the house. Everybody has to step over him to get inside or out.

A couple of men nod at me when I go by, and I nod back. Their faces say they feel sorry for me. I stick my hands in the pockets of my dress and scoot by people, wishing I could have stayed at the river all night. Even on normal days I don't like being the center of attention. Max thumps his tail twice against the wooden porch as I pass, as if only pretending to be asleep. After I pet him, I go inside looking around for my family. The crowd is as thick as church on Easter Sunday, except without any hope of resurrection.

The first people I see when I go inside are Preacher and his wife sitting in the living room. I have to resist grabbing him by the lapels and tossing him out of Daddy's chair. He takes a neatly folded white handkerchief out of his coat pocket to soak up the sweat from his forehead. For someone who has a guarantee of going to heaven, he sure does sweat a lot.

Preacher motions for me to come over. "Your Daddy's one of the fortunate to get to go to the Great Beyond so young," he says.

"I wish people would quit saying that," I say. "What exactly is he beyond?"

Preacher's eyes widen like I haven't heard a word he's said every Sunday service since I was a little girl. "Well, he's in heaven, of course. He's in a better place. He's *beyond* this earthly place. "

"What could be better than sitting here amongst all his family and friends?" I ask.

Preachers face turns red and Amy's look tells me I'd better just drop it.

Amy sits squashed between Aunt Chloe and Uncle John, who are both big people. She looks about as miserable as I feel. I walked past their latest new Buick on the road below the house. It looks bigger than the last one, probably to accommodate their size.

Amy nibbles on her fingernails like she does when she's nervous. Every corner of our house has people crammed in it, with no place for the shyest McAllister to hide.

Aunt Chloe is Mama's younger sister and she lives with her husband in Rocky Bluff. My hope is to duck into the kitchen unnoticed, but when Aunt Chloe sees me she hauls herself off the sofa and comes over and hugs me like I am her long lost relative. I let her do it, even though she wears enough perfume to choke a goat. The smell always makes my eyes water and sticks to my skin and clothes. Whenever she comes over for Sunday dinner, her scent lingers in the house well into Tuesday. In the privacy of our bedroom, my sisters and I call it *Ode to Toilet Water*.

"Louisa May, we've been worried about you," Aunt Chloe says. Before I can get away she pulls me into her, and I hold my breath like I am diving into the deep part of the river. After she releases me I tell her that I am fine, which of course is the lie of the century.

Aunt Chloe's eyes are bloodshot and I wonder if that is from crying over Daddy or from her perfume, which is especially strong tonight. Chloe has had an easier life than Mama. Chloe's husband, my Uncle John, owns a furniture store in Rocky Bluff and makes a good living. They never had any children.

"I just can't think of anything more horrible than what's happened to your daddy," Aunt Chloe continues. She sniffs back tears and plucks a lace handkerchief from her cleavage.

"I'd better check on Mama," I say, stepping away before Aunt Chloe has a chance to hug me again.

In the bedroom, wall to wall people stand around talking about Daddy in whispers. From the look of him, you can't even tell he's been in an accident. All the blood is cleaned up and one of Aunt Sadie's beautiful quilts covers the bed, the one with the hummingbirds sewn on each corner. Besides selling mountain remedies and blackberry wine, Aunt Sadie—like Mama—makes quilts to sell to city people, though Sadie is much better than Mama when it comes to making quilts. Mary Jane's grandmother in Little Rock bought one from her when she came to visit two summers ago, and she paid Sadie fifty dollars for it. After that, some of her Little Rock, high-society friends wanted one, too. Sadie manages to make one quilt every winter and has a waiting list seven years long, all the way into 1947.

I try to hide my shock at seeing Daddy laid out on the bed. He is wearing his Sunday shoes and his only suit, the suit he wore to every funeral and wedding in Katy's Ridge, and the suit he always complained about how stiff and uncomfortable it was.

"How dare you make him wear that," I say to Mama over the whispers. "He should be wearing a pair of overalls and his favorite flannel shirt if he has to wear them for all eternity."

I feel bad now for running off to the river and not making sure things were done right.

The voices in the room go silent and a dozen set of eyes look at me like I've just killed Daddy myself.

In a matter of seconds, the look on Mama's face changes from all-consuming grief to fuming anger.

"She's just distraught," somebody says in my defense.

I recognize the voice as Miss Mildred who plays the organ at the church. In the past, I've spent a fair amount of time making fun of Miss Mildred and realize now that I will have to stop, since she spoke up for me.

Not the best organ player, Miss Mildred's hymns are riddled with bad notes that sound like little farts. I have spent my entire childhood swallowing giggles as fast as her little organ farts come out. Some of us learned that you can swallow air and make little farts, too. The boys are really good at this, which guarantees more giggles. If Mama's cold looks don't stop me from rolling all hysterical down the church aisle, I force myself to think of Jesus on the cross.

In the next instant I feel guilty for thinking about farts while Daddy is laying dead. But then I figure that he might find it funny, too. However, the wrath of Mama sobers me quick, as she pulls me through the crowd and outside to a corner of the porch where no one can hear us.

"What do you think you're doing?" Mama says. Her whispered words come out like shouts. "Have you no respect for the dead?"

"*The dead* is Daddy," I say.

She takes a step back like I've just slapped her hard in the face.

Sadie's dog, Max, comes over and sniffs my crotch, as if this is the only comfort he has to offer, given the blessing out I am about to receive.

"Louisa May McAllister, this is how things are done when someone dies and you *will* respect it or you will be cleaning out the outhouse for the rest of your natural life. Do you hear me?"

I smile, grateful that Mama is taking me down a peg because it makes me not feel so much like an orphan. She narrows her eyes at my smile.

"Yes, ma'am," I say. "I will respect how things are done."

She lifts her head as though proud of winning this battle and I follow her back into the house to pay our respects to Daddy. The crowd parts as Mama makes her way back to the rocking chair next to the bed, the chair where all we babies got rocked, me being the last. This rocker is more like a family member than of a piece of furniture and creaks out a tune on the wooden floors as sweet as any Daddy might have played on the banjo. It will probably be the chair that rocks all the grandbabies, too.

While it is easy to imagine Jo, Amy and Meg having babies and bringing them here to be rocked in the family chair, it is much harder to imagine myself doing it. I've already decided that I'll have babies only after I've finished all the fun things in life, like going on adventures and exploring a world bigger than Katy's Ridge.

Besides all the other things Aunt Sadie does, she also works as a midwife here in Katy's Ridge. I've gone with her a few times on a delivery. Mainly I take care of the younger kids in the family, if there are any. But I've heard enough hollering coming out of bedrooms to wonder if babies are worth all the pain they bring with them.

Contrite as the best Baptist, I make my way back through the crowded room. People nod as if to acknowledge the effort I am making. Even with the window open the room is stuffy. It isn't big enough for this many people. When I reach the bed I touch Daddy's hand and then yank it away. It is cold, like something in the icebox. Before I can stop them, tears rush to my eyes. The last thing I want to do is cry in front of all these people so I sniff them back so hard I feel a rush of air in my eyeballs.

After I slide in beside her, Mama puts her arm around my waist and anchors me in place as Mr. Blackstone, Daddy's boss at the sawmill, tells her how much Daddy will be missed.

"You're very kind," Mama replies.

"You're very kind," I echo, trying to match Mama's tone.

Mr. Blackstone's daughter, Becky, is four years ahead of me in school. Seeing him this close I now know where Becky gets her big nose because her father has one just like it. Their eyes are alike, too, small and narrow. The only inconsistency being that Mr. Blackstone is practically bald and Becky's hair is long and straight.

"I don't know how we can ever replace him," Mr. Blackstone concludes.

Mama thanks him again for his kindness and squeezes me like I am not to repeat it. If she resents Mr. Blackstone at all for Daddy's accident she doesn't let on, although I heard her say to Daddy more than once that Mr. Blackstone is cheap and hasn't hired enough men for all the logging that needs to get done.

Before he leaves, Mr. Blackstone shakes the tips of my fingers like he is afraid to touch my whole hand, which irritates me to no end. Before I have time to react, Mama shoots me a look that would stop a full grown mountain lion in its tracks. In the meantime, I do my best to ignore the body lying on the bed in the clothes Daddy would have burned if she let him.

"Where are your sisters?" Mama asks.

"I think Jo and Meg are in the kitchen," I say. "And Amy's keeping Aunt Chloe and Uncle John company."

"Why don't you go help Jo and Meg," she says, releasing her arm from my waist.

Mama's answer for everything that ails a person is hard work. For her, life is just one big chore with no end. Daddy always said she was stubborn as an ox, and she plowed to the end of the row of everything she did. He said we girls would be grateful for that trait someday. Though I don't see how gratitude and working like an ox are related at all.

As I'm leaving, I glance at the old photograph Mama always keeps on her dresser. She never talks about her past. Her parents came over from Germany, but we've not heard one story about them. I've spent some time studying that photograph. The grandparents I never met are standing on a small rug out in a dirt yard, somewhere in Germany, dressed up in front of a Hansel and Gretel house. They look stern, not a bit of happiness on their faces. Aunt Chloe never talks about them either, but sometimes I hear Mama and Chloe talking in German together in the kitchen when they don't think anybody else is listening.

Before leaving the room, I turn and look over at Daddy. I just keep thinking that any minute he will sit up and ask why all these people are in our house. When he hears the story of how we all thought he was dead, he'll probably laugh so loud it can be heard in the next valley. Wishful thinking comes in handy if you want to keep reality from sinking in too fast.

My fantasy fades when I notice my father's arms have been folded neatly across his chest. He could be sleeping except for that. Nobody sleeps that way. Maybe that's why people do it. So mourners won't go poking around on dead people expecting them to wake up.

The kitchen is crowded and busy like Thanksgiving dinner is being made. All sorts of food sits on the kitchen table that people have brought, but Jo and Meg are making more. Every burner on our old stove has something cooking, as well as the oven, and the kitchen is hot as Hades. Jo peels potatoes by the sink and still looks fresh, no matter how hot it is. It doesn't seem fair sometimes that she can be so beautiful and the rest of us are so plain. What makes it all right is that Jo doesn't seem to know how pretty she is.

"Where have you been?" Jo says to me in the doorway. "We were worried about you."

I can tell she's been crying. "I was down by the river," I say. "I needed some time alone."

"That's what we figured," she says. She dabs a tiny offering of sweat from her forehead onto her sleeve.

In contrast to Jo, Meg looks wilted as she slumps over the kitchen counter cutting dough into biscuits. Her face is still splotched like she has broken out in hives from all the sadness.

"Mama said I should help," I say to Jo.

Sweat trickles down my back, all the way to the elastic in my underwear. I still have on my everyday school dress but nobody seems to care. Luckily, I found my shoes on the way home, so at least I'm not barefooted.

"You could mix the egg salad." Jo points over to the countertop where a bowl waits.

"Why are we cooking so much food?" I ask.

"All these people have to eat something," she says, sounding a little bit like Mama.

"But there's tons of food already here," I say.

"We might run out," Jo says.

Aunt Sadie pulls me in for a hug as she makes tea at the stove. Her eyes look sad and I can tell she's done her fair share of crying, too.

"How are you holding up, sweetheart?" she asks.

I shrug and she pulls me in for another hug. Unlike Aunt Chloe's hugs, I don't mind Sadie's at all. She smells like molasses and I wonder if she's been making one of her tonics because she often adds molasses to disguise the bitter taste of roots and whatnot.

Amy walks into the kitchen, finally free of Aunt Chloe and Uncle John. She stirs something on the stove and doesn't talk to any of us. You never know what Amy is thinking or feeling because it never makes its way out of her mouth, you just have to guess. My guess is that Amy is as devastated as any of us. It's just all bottled up inside. Amy and Mama are alike in that way. Except Amy isn't as good as Mama at pretending nothing is wrong.

Aunt Sadie fills the pitcher with tea to take back to the living room. She put sprigs of mint in it that float on the top. I want to ask her if Daddy can still see us and hear us, or if he is somewhere in heaven cut off from the rest of us here. I trust Aunt Sadie to tell me the truth. But she is gone before I can ask.

I mash the boiled eggs with a fork and remember how much I hate cooking. I'd rather be doing a hundred other things, most of which are outdoors. I don't mind eating, though. Daddy and I both love to eat. I keep thinking of him lying there in their bed and wonder if Doc Lester even knows how to take a proper pulse. For all we know Daddy just passed out and nobody thought to wake him.

Miss Mildred comes into the kitchen, fanning herself with a piece of music she pulled from her purse.

"I'll play something real pretty for your daddy at the service tomorrow," Miss Mildred says to Jo.

"Thank you, Miss Mildred," Jo says. She glances over at me, her eyes wide. We both know Miss Mildred's best intentions don't always play out.

Daddy's favorite hymn was *Amazing Grace*. It wasn't unusual for him to go around all day on a Saturday singing that song over and over again while he helped Mama. He always liked the church hymns where somebody was lost, then got found. Unlike the people in those hymns, I've never known him to get lost. He knows every nook and cranny of Katy's Ridge and he could tell you the name of every tree, wildflower, bird or animal because he studied them in a book. He probably could have been a professor at a big college if he wanted to, but Daddy found himself here in Katy's Ridge and made the best of it.

While I mash eggs with a fork, odd thoughts pop into my mind, like I hope Daddy won't have to wait in line in heaven like the one time we went to the picture show in Rocky Bluff. A war is going on overseas and I wonder how God deals with a whole bunch of people showing up at heaven's gate all at once.

"When will they move him to the church?" I ask Miss Mildred, since she seems to be the only one talking about what will happen next.

"Probably first thing in the morning," she whispers, like it is a secret.

I've only been to one other funeral that I remember—old Mr. Williams, who was cranky all the time and walked with a cane. Nobody liked him. He complained about everything under the sun, and if he didn't like something about you he'd tell you right to your face. He called me *Miss Wiggle Worm* when I was a little girl, because I didn't sit still enough in church. On this subject, Mama probably agreed. People paid their respects to Mr. Williams, yet even his widow walked lighter after he was gone.

At his funeral, Preacher said that Mr. Williams had gone on to the *Great Beyond*, this being one of Preacher's favorite sayings, and he kept pointing to a crack in the ceiling of the church like the crack was a pipeline into heaven. This proved God's goodness, as far as I was concerned, if he let crotchety Mr. Williams into heaven.

Daddy's death feels worlds different. People whisper and watch us, as if they secretly wonder what our family did to deserve such bad luck. The whispers stop whenever me or my sisters or Mama come into the room.

"Louisa May, watch what you're doing," Jo says.

Pieces of egg fall on the kitchen table and I apologize and shove the egg back into the bowl.

"Maybe you should go outside for awhile." Jo twists her hair up in the back as if to let in cooler air, and then lets it drop.

I agree and go outside. As the youngest McAllister, I am often treated like the baby of the family. Even though last summer I took on some of Daddy's lankiness and height, this hasn't translated into my family seeing me at all different.

On the porch a different bunch are standing, people from Katy's Ridge I don't see for months at a time. It's hot for October, more like mid-July, but now the breeze is cooler, like the breeze from the river has finally made it up here.

A chill goes through me just thinking about what winter will be like without Daddy here to get us ready for it. He splits and gets in the wood and bundles us up for school and fixes our snowshoes whenever the snow is too deep for regular shoes. To avoid the sadness that comes with it, I shake these thoughts away like snow from a tree branch.

Almost everybody in Katy's Ridge is here in my front yard. Horatio Sector and his wife and their kids stand away from everybody else, in a little huddle. Nobody pays them no mind. The worst you can do to people is to pretend they don't exist. But the Sectors are friends of Daddy's that have come to pay their respects. I let the others stare and walk over to them like Daddy would have done.

"Thanks for coming," I say to Mr. Sector, who holds their youngest boy's hand.

"Your father was a good man, Miss Wildflower," he says.

Mr. Sector is part Cherokee, though he is dark enough to be whole. He and his family live downriver of Katy's Ridge and keep to themselves. People aren't that friendly to him or his family except for Daddy. I walk down with Daddy sometimes to buy honey off of Mr. Sector and they will sit and talk away most of the afternoon. Mr. Sector is married to a white woman named June and they have a bunch of children. None of them come to school, but even the youngest child can read as well as me. They read Cherokee, too, which I hope to learn someday.

Nobody can figure out why Mr. Sector's cornfield is always about a foot taller than other people's. His bees make a ton more honey, too. Some people say that June Sector is a witch, but I think ignorant people say whatever they think will be the most hurtful. June has blond hair and the children are a mixture of the two of them. Some have blue eyes, some have black, and their skin ranges in tone from golden honey to almost white.

Mr. Sector hands me a small leather pouch with something inside. I pull out a stone the size of a half-dollar that glimmers red from the torches burning in the yard.

"It's beautiful," I say.

"It's a ruby," Mr. Sector says. "I found it myself."

"I'll make sure Mama gets it," I say and thank him.

"No, miss," he hesitates, "it's for you."

I look up at him like he must have made a mistake.

"You and Mister Joseph were very close. This is to help fill the empty space in your heart."

Though it's nearly impossible, I hold back my tears and shake his hand. Some of the men turn to watch, as if touching an Indian's hand is breaking the law and I might get arrested.

"Mister Joseph was very kind to us," Jane Sector says.

I thank her and shake her hand, as well. Then I excuse myself and go over to sit on the porch steps. The heaviness of the evening makes me tired and I want to cry. The whole community is grieving for Daddy, but I'm not so sure I want to share him this way.

Max moves to the dirt next to Mama's flowerbeds and when I go over to pet him he licks my hand. Kids I know are in the crowd but they look away and step into the shadows, talking amongst themselves. By the light of one of the torches I can see Johnny Monroe and his sisters with big plates of food standing next to their father, Arthur Monroe. It would be just like the Monroes to come just for the food. They mainly keep to themselves, but in a different way than the Sectors. The people in Katy's Ridge hate the Sectors because Mr. Sector is an Indian and different. But Arthur Monroe doesn't just hate the Sectors, he hates everybody.

Ruby Monroe looks sad tonight, but she always looks sad. Johnny stands between Ruby and his younger sister, Melody. Their clothes are dirty and they look as though they haven't bathed in days.

Moments later Mary Jane and her brother Victor come up the hill with their parents. It feels like a hundred years since I've seen Mary Jane, even though it was earlier that day. Her mother speaks first, telling me how sorry she is about my father. Then her parents walk inside and Mary Jane and Victor stay outside with me. The three of us stand there for a while, like we don't know what to say. Victor draws marks in the dirt with his shoe and keeps his hands in his pockets. His hair looks wet, like he washed it right before he came. Victor is one of Max's favorite people and old Max jumps up on him and pushes at him with his nose.

"He likes you," I say.

"Everybody likes Victor," Mary Jane says.

"It's a curse," Victor says and smiles.

It is good to see a smile amongst all these sad faces, but Victor looks embarrassed by it and stops. He plays some with Max.

"We're going out back, big brother," Mary Jane says.

"Okay," he says, grabbing a stick to throw to Max.

Mary Jane tugs at my dress sleeve and we walk around to the back porch. People have gathered on the back porch, too. Some are standing, some sitting, and not a single stray cat in sight. They probably won't come out from under the house for days after this.

We take one of the lanterns off the end of the porch and go up past the outhouse to sit on a boulder Mary Jane and I used to play on when we were little. I steady the lantern, making sure it won't fall off and leave us sitting in the dark. When we were younger, we used to pretend this boulder was the broad back of a humped back whale. We sailed out to sea in our imaginations, sailing the waters of oceans far away. I wish I could do that now for real. I want to be a thousand, maybe even a million miles away from what has happened. I need time to think, to get this right in my mind, without a lot of people around.

Below us the house looks spooky. People are like shadows with pipes and cigarettes lighting up the dark hillside like fireflies.

"This is strange, your daddy dying like this," Mary Jane says finally.

"Much more than strange," I say. We let the silence gather around us. I can tell she is uncomfortable. But at the same time I am grateful she is making an effort. Even though we've been friends since we were in diapers, neither one of us have ever gone through anything like this before. If this had happened to Mary Jane's father I wouldn't know what to say to her, either.

"Everybody in Katy's Ridge must be here," she says.

"It looks like it," I say.

Down the hill toward the house I see Jo washing dishes through the kitchen window. I feel guilty for not helping, but I am grateful to be here with my friend.

"Everybody liked him," she says.

"Yeah, I think they did."

Night noises surround us: crickets, toads, lizards and other small critters moving around in the fallen leaves. Do they mourn when one of their own dies?

"He was always helping people out," she says, as if this is something I don't know. "I liked him, too," she says softly.

Mary Jane and I have never been this awkward together for a day in our lives.

"How's your mother taking this?" she asks.

"Pretty good, I guess."

We sit for a long time, not saying much of anything.

"I'm so sorry," Mary Jane says. Then she buries her head in her dress and starts to bawl, complete with snot. I pat her back to comfort her. I have never seen Mary Jane cry like this, and I wish she'd just stop it. My father is laid out in the bedroom and the entire population of Katy's Ridge is at our house, even the Monroes and the Sectors, and it is taking everything I have to hold myself together. The last thing I need is people falling apart right in front of me, especially my best friend.

To my relief, Mary Jane finally stops weeping and wipes a long, slimy trail of snot on the sleeve of her dress. But I guess her crying is better than ignoring me, like the other kids from our school. They act like I have a fatal disease they might catch if they get too close.

Later that night after everybody has eaten and paid their respects to our family, the house starts to empty out. I walk with Mary Jane and Victor to the bottom of the hill. Somebody has put lanterns every few feet along the path so that people can see how to get home. The new moon is no help tonight and the wind blows at the lanterns, trying to put them out. The wind makes the trees creak and moan, as if they miss Daddy, too.

We say our goodbyes, and I walk back up the hill, passing the last of the people going home. When I get to the front porch Mama is standing at the railing looking out into the dark night.

"It was a good crowd," she says.

Since I don't know what else to say, I agree, and feel more tired-out than I've ever been in my life. I leave her standing in the shadows and go inside. The screen door slams shut behind me. Any other day Mama would yell at me for letting the door slam, and I half-wish she'd yell at me now so everything would feel normal, but she doesn't. The truth is I doubt that life will ever feel the same again.

This is about the time of evening Daddy would be picking up his banjo to pick out his version of a lullaby, while my sisters and I get ready for bed. For once it doesn't bother me that my sisters and I all sleep in one room. After Meg and I came along, Daddy built a small bed in the corner for us next to the big bed in the center that Jo and Amy shared. Because of the small room, we bump elbows when the four of us get on our nightgowns. In spite of the ways they bother me sometimes, I love my sisters. Being the youngest, in one way or another, they all look out for me.

Any other night we'd be talking or laughing before we went to bed, but tonight we are quiet. Meg and I crawl over Jo and Amy to get to our corner of the room like we do every night. In a way it helps to know that I am not the only one left behind.

In the meantime, I haven't given up on a miracle. If Jesus is all that Preacher makes him out to be, I don't see why he can't do for Daddy what he did for Lazarus. Preacher is always bringing Lazarus back to life and it appears to be one of his favorite sermons. He especially likes to point out that Lazarus started to rot before Jesus found him. I force myself not to think about Daddy rotting, even though he and I have always been fascinated with nature's way of decomposing dead things. I get on my knees and pray for a Lazarus-sized miracle instead.

"Jo, where's Mama going to sleep?" I say, suddenly alarmed by the thought of Daddy stretched out on their bed.

"Aunt Sadie made up a bed on the couch," she says.

"Mama probably won't sleep tonight anyway," Meg says.

"I probably won't either," Amy agrees.

"Well, I will," Jo says, turning off the lights. "I'm too sad and exhausted to stay awake."

"Who would have thought people could eat that much?" Meg says from the darkness. "And they brought things, too. Daddy would make some joke that we'll have leftovers for the next two years."

I haven't eaten all day except for breakfast, and I still don't feel hungry at all. It's as if the sadness from the day filled me up like a full-course meal.

"I think Aunt Chloe filled her plate at least three times," Amy says, giggling. She stops herself and apologizes, but then Meg starts giggling, too. Before long we are all laughing into our pillows or bed-covers or whatever we can find. It feels bad and good at the same time. Laughter gives me hope. Until then, I felt dead like Daddy. We laugh at nothing and everything all at once and decide that if Daddy were here he'd be laughing, too.

We settle back into our beds and I can hear Mama and Aunt Sadie talking softly in the living room. For the first time in our lives, Mama doesn't come in to say goodnight, and she hasn't even scolded us for making noise.

I close my eyes and pretend that nothing has changed. I wait on Daddy to come in and read us part of whatever book he's been reading. Sometimes it is *Robinson Crusoe* or *Moby Dick* or something from the Old Testament where so-and-so begets so-and-so. Those are the nights we fall asleep the fastest.

Everything grows quiet, then. The quietness feels as deep as the deepest part of Sutter's Lake, the part of the lake where I can't see or touch the bottom, no matter how much I hold my breath and dive. I can't stop thinking of Daddy's body in the next room. It wouldn't be like him to haunt a place. He didn't believe in ghosts, no matter how many spooky stories we girls made up to scare him.

After a while Meg starts to cry. I rub her shoulders and back for the longest time, like Daddy always did if we didn't feel well. Afterwards, I close my eyes and think of the river, its waves lapping against the shoreline. In my imagination, a water bug skims on the top. They keep their balance no matter what the water is doing underneath them. I try to be that water bug and let the waves of emotion pass under me without getting capsized.

Meg's crying keeps up until her breathing finally deepens into sleep. In a room filled with sisters, I feel totally alone. In my loneliness, I think of Jesus on the cross when he asked God why he abandoned him. For all I know, I've been praying for miracles from somebody that doesn't even exist. Too tired to question things anymore, the worst day of my life ends when, at last, I fall asleep.

CHAPTER TEN

The morning of the funeral I smell breakfast before I open my eyes. I smile at the thought of Daddy and Mama in the kitchen with their first cup of coffee, then I remember that he won't be there. When I walk by the door to their bedroom it is closed, like he is still sleeping. But the nightmare of the day before is true. The accident really happened. He is really gone.

When I come into the kitchen Aunt Sadie gives me one of her big, strong hugs. She has made a breakfast of eggs, bacon and biscuits.

"I want you to drink this," she says. "It'll keep your strength up."

A glass of something dark green sits on the kitchen counter. All of Aunt Sadie's concoctions taste like tree bark and grass mixed together, but I don't argue with her, I just drink it and hold my nose while I swallow.

We all sit around the kitchen table as if we are in a daze. Jo looks like she's been crying again and Amy is quiet, as usual, and Meg stares into her coffee cup. Even Mama has stopped her busyness and is nursing a cup of coffee. Despite all the sadness weighing down the room, the smell of the bacon reminds me of how hungry I am. Before I know it, I've eaten two eggs, three strips of bacon, and two biscuits with butter and some of Horatio Sector's honey on it.

Just as I finish breakfast a knock comes at the front door and Mama answers it. Men's voices fill the living room. Some of Daddy's friends are here with a pine box in the yard behind them. I smell the wood all the way from the living room.

"I was up all night making it," Silas Magee says. "I think it's the best I've ever done."

Silas is the best carpenter anywhere. He made practically everything we own. Between him and Daddy our family has enough wood and kindling stacked next to the porch to get us through two hard winters.

Mama thanks Silas and the other men but has that faraway look in her eyes again like she might climb in the box with Daddy if given half a chance.

"We need to get him down the hill," Silas says. "Doc Lester has that contraption he bought waiting on the road."

Mama steps aside as the men carry the coffin into the house. Her eyes are fixed on the pine box and when I try to follow the men she holds me back.

"Come on," Jo says from behind me. "Let's go pick flowers for the church." As the oldest, Jo has taken over Mama's job of telling us sisters what to do.

Meg and Amy follow Jo and me out the back door to the path into the woods behind our house. As we walk, I picture Daddy being carried down the hill by the same men who carried him up.

"Will they take him right to the church?" I ask Jo.

"I believe so," she says, locking her arm in mine.

"Will Mama go, too?"

"Probably," she says. "At least for a little while, to make sure everything's set up the way she wants."

We walk to the sunny side of the hill to search for flowers. Early that summer there were daffodils in bloom, and crocuses, white trillium and crested irises. But now, in early fall, there is only snakeroot, goldenrod, asters and witch hazel. A few crested irises risk a late bloom but they are scrawny compared to weeks before. We gather what we can find, along with fern fronds and take them back to the kitchen and put them in water. Amy will arrange them since she is good at things like that.

The men and Daddy are gone when we get back to the house. For the first time that I can remember, Daddy is on his way to church without us, and something about that makes a lump of grief lodge in my throat.

Every Sunday, rain or shine, freezing cold or summer heat, we walk as a family to the Katy's Ridge Missionary Baptist church, the only church in Katy's Ridge. The cornerstone outside the church kitchen has the date 1911 chiseled into it. Rocky Bluff, the biggest town close to us, has four churches: one Methodist, one Presbyterian, and two more Baptist churches—one being a Baptist church for colored people. Aunt Sadie says the colored people praise Jesus by singing, clapping their hands and dancing in the aisles. That comes closer to my idea of what a church should be. But the coloreds and the whites stay apart in these parts, except for Aunt Sadie who goes to worship with them every now and again, whenever she's invited.

In the past, on days when the temperature fell below freezing, I didn't see why we couldn't skip the freezing walk and just talk to God from in front of our warm wood stove. God made winter in the first place, so why wouldn't he understand? Daddy could have led us in some hymns and Mama could have read from the Bible, some of the good parts that Preacher never got around to, like what love meant to the Corinthians.

Most Sundays, Preacher talks about Satan and the evils of sin and how we have to repent. He says we are all sinners and no matter how hard we try to be good people we can't keep from sinning. What I never figured out was if people were so horrible already, what was there to aim for? Daddy didn't like it when I questioned Preacher, especially to his face. But I could tell he didn't go along with everything Preacher said, either. Sometimes he would doze off right in the middle of the sermon. When this happened, I was supposed to nudge him awake before Mama noticed.

I am glad it is fall because the church in winter is always too hot or too cold, nothing in between. Preacher's nephew, Gordon, gets a dollar a month to stoke the coal furnace in the basement of the church, and so we either roast like we are already in the fires of hell or freeze like explorers in the Antarctic. But it is warm enough today that maybe some of the windows can be opened and a good breeze let in.

After Mama comes back home, we sit around the kitchen table finishing off an apple pie sharing two forks between us. We are waiting for three o'clock when we are to head to the church. Nobody talks about the empty seat where Daddy usually sits, or how we are supposed to go on with this big empty chair in our lives.

Meg chatters away about nothing and Amy never says a word. Jo and Aunt Sadie stay close to Mama, like she is a daisy whose petals might all fall off at once. Time drags on like a wagon stuck in the mud, a wagon that we're all too sad to get out and push. The red rooster clock over the icebox ticks so loud we can hear it whenever the talking stops. It doesn't seem we'll ever get to where we are going, not that any of us want to go there anyway.

I excuse myself and go out to the front porch to read in the sun. Two stray cats that have been hanging out at the house since Daddy fed them supper scraps, keep me company. I try to concentrate on a passage in *Oliver Twist* that Daddy and I were reading together two days before, but I read the same paragraph three times without understanding it once.

Aunt Sadie comes to the back door. "It's time to get ready," she says.

I have a thousand questions for Aunt Sadie but my mouth has stopped working just like my mind. I nod and come in the house.

I am the last to take a bath. We take our baths on the back porch in Mama's biggest washtub, except in winter. Right now it is just warm enough for us not to freeze to death, as long as Aunt Sadie keeps the hot water coming that is boiling on the stove. Two kettles of boiling water and a bucket of cold usually get the temperature just right.

We can't afford indoor plumbing yet because we have to hire the men with the things they need to lay the pipes all the way up our hill. But the electric lines were easier, so we've had power for a few years. Mary Jane has indoor plumbing and so does just about everybody else, except for maybe the Monroes, the Sectors and us. The money in the Mason jar just hasn't been enough.

The only fight I ever saw Mama and Daddy have was about Daddy always putting a portion of our jar money into the offering at church. Mama thinks an indoor toilet is more important than Preacher having a new robe to wear at baptisms and she told Daddy so. She said he'd give away our last dime if somebody asked for it, which is probably true.

Aunt Sadie hangs sheets around the bathtub for privacy since my body has started to change. I am going from being a girl to becoming a young woman, and though my sisters and I share a bedroom and have seen each other naked, I still feel shy.

Undressing quickly, I rub the soap over the goose bumps on my arms and legs and then wash my hair and rinse it with a pitcher of water nearby. Aunt Sadie brings out a towel, stiff from hanging on the line, and it softens as I wrap it around my shoulders. I shudder and shake until I put on my underwear, slip and then the dress I will wear to the funeral.

At the kitchen table, Aunt Sadie helps comb the tangles out of my hair, instead of Mama, and I thank God for small blessings until I remember how angry I am that he hasn't produced any miracles yet.

While everybody else gets ready, I wait in the living room. Daddy's banjo looks lonely just sitting there. Does it miss him? Do the strings hanker to be touched by him again, the frets wait to be turned and tuned? The house seems quiet in a way I can't put my finger on. I study the difference until it hits me that a voice is missing. A baritone voice to balance out all the sopranos. Daddy's voice.

We leave the house going down the path that Daddy's body traveled earlier that morning. Mama, Jo, and Aunt Sadie lead the way, followed by Amy, Meg, and me carrying bunches of wildflowers and ferns. I wear new shoes that scrape against my heels and I can already tell I am going to have a whopper of a blister. Aunt Chloe brought new shoes for all of us that morning and dropped them off when we were picking flowers. In the past, Mama would have refused such charity, even from her sister. But she doesn't seem to have the energy to argue right now.

Aunt Sadie has not left Mama's side. As Daddy's sister, she must have a deep sadness all her own, though other than those first moments when she found out, she hasn't let it show. She just watches out for Mama, because that's what her brother probably would want her to do.

"Daddy will like being the center of attention," Meg says, the first to break the silence.

"Who'd want attention that way?" I say, irked by her dreaminess.

"Remember, we're going to celebrate his life, not his death," Aunt Sadie says.

"It sure doesn't feel like a celebration," I say.

"I know it doesn't," Aunt Sadie says. "It's just what we say so it won't hurt so bad. But I guess nothing could help with that."

She drops back a few steps and puts her arm around me, squeezing my shoulder. I think of Daddy hugging me the day before, when I came into the kitchen for breakfast. If I'd known it would be the last time we hugged, I would have hung on longer, instead of wanting to get to Mama's biscuits.

Sadie moves back to Mama's side and we walk the rest of the way without saying much. Instead of almost twelve, I feel like a little girl again. I kick a rock down the side of the road, something I might have done years ago.

The first thing we see when we near the church is Doc Lester's hearse.

"That is the tackiest contraption I have ever laid eyes on," I say, using the word I heard Silas Magee use earlier.

"He bought it used in Rocky Bluff from the colored people's funeral home," Meg says. She always knows the details of what's going on.

"He must have shined it up special," I say, "because it looks like a brand new copper penny." It sits in front of the church, too fancy for the dinky little building. "Daddy always made fun of that hearse," I continue. "He said if Doc couldn't cure you, he could always drive you away in his hearse. Either way he got paid."

"Louisa May," Mama says, "must you always say exactly what's on your mind." She sighs like I have crawled all over her grief wearing dirty shoes.

What Mama doesn't know, is that the thought of Daddy in Doc Lester's funeral wagon makes me want to cry and hit somebody at the same time, so she's lucky I'm just talking.

The same people from the night before stand around outside the church. Some turn to watch us come down the road. I imagine *Onward Christian Soldiers* playing in the background because we walk like soldiers going to war.

Mama reaches over and takes my hand as we come to the church, like all is forgiven regarding the earlier hearse comments, and I nearly cry from the unexpected tenderness.

"Don't worry, Louisa May, we're going to be fine," Mama says. She squeezes my hand.

"I promise to be strong, Mama," I say and squeeze hers back.

At that moment I feel close to her, something I don't feel too often. But as quickly as it comes, it goes, and she drops my hand.

"Right this way, Mrs. McAllister," Preacher says to Mama. He usually calls her Nell, but today he uses her married name.

He leads us to the entrance of the church like we've never been there before. We follow him inside and Jo puts the flowers on the coffin while we take our places on the front row. Miss Mildred starts playing the organ and we are sitting so close we can hear her feet pumping the slats at the bottom that makes the low notes. She hums along, pushing her glasses up on her nose again and again, studying the music intently, as if trying to do an extra special job. She hits sour notes that a week ago would have made me swallow my hysterics, but today I don't feel like laughing.

The pine box with Daddy in it sits at the front of the church. Pots of lilies are placed on either end of Preacher's podium which is moved over to the side. The casket lid is off but we can't see anything. I imagine Daddy sitting up and giving us a wave, a modern-day Lazarus, giving the whole church the shock of a lifetime. I wait, sending God the message that this would be the perfect time to prove his greatness. In exchange, I promise not to be mad at him anymore and then cross my fingers, arms, and legs for good luck.

Miss Mildred's solo goes on forever and I pass the time by re-membering the only other time I sat on the front row in church. It was the day I got baptized at eight years of age. If you had the un-fortunate luck to be nine and still unsaved, people in Katy's Ridge stared at you during altar calls, those times when Preacher invited the unsaved to play on God's team. Once tapped on the shoulder by

Jesus, you were to ask him to come into your heart and be your personal Savior. It seemed a regular Savior would be good enough for me, but as far as I can tell, the Baptist's insist on a *personal* one.

That Sunday I walked down the aisle, trying to make up some tears like Audrey Fisher had the week before, proof that Jesus touched my heart. I liked Jesus just fine, but I hated being stared at, so I tapped Jesus on the shoulder instead of him tapping me just to get the busy-bodies of Katy's Ridge off my back. To make matters worse, when I stood at the altar, Preacher put his hands on my head and prayed for my salvation so long a big drop of sweat fell from his head onto mine. As a result, I bolted upright in complete disgust only to be pushed down again while he kept praying.

The next Sunday Preacher dunked me and Jake Turner—who was two years ahead of me in school and who people had already worried had gone to the Devil—at the place in the river where it is shallow enough to stand in and get dunked from the waist backwards. As soon as we were up out of the water, Preacher announced Jake and me were full of the Holy Spirit. I kept waiting to feel different, maybe a little lightheaded or something, but mainly I just felt wet.

At the very least I thought an angel should appear and give me a message of some sort. But nothing happened, except I found out why people don't walk around in wet clothes. It is not the least bit comfortable. My dress kept sticking to me and my underwear twisted up so bad I started to get the underwear version of a rope burn. After we dried off, Jake and I sat on the front row of the church and told our testimonies to the whole congregation. This was when I was supposed to say how rotten and lost I was before God shined a light on me and changed my heart forever. These testimonies always made

Preacher smile from ear to ear and nod his head and rock back and for on his dusty black shoes saying "Amen" with every sentence.

Even Jake Turner came up with something good to say about how he would never look at Katy's Ridge the same way again. But I felt like a colossal fake because as far as I could see, nothing had happened to me. I felt the same as I always had, which wasn't good or bad, but just the same. Despite my total lack of revelation, I made up something about how I had suddenly seen the light about how sinful it was to talk back to my mother and pick my nose in public. The last part made Jake Turner laugh. I don't know what made me walk up to the altar in the first place, except to keep from getting stared at.

The ferns and flowers we picked look nice and give me something to look at while we wait for Miss Mildred to finish playing the organ. When she finally stops, she smiles over at Mama as Preacher walks up to the podium with his Bible in his hand. Preacher is never without his Bible. He holds onto it like it is glued to his fingers. I wonder sometimes if his wife has to yank it out of his hands at night after he falls asleep.

"Dearly beloved," Preacher starts out, like we are at a wedding instead of a funeral. "We are gathered here today to celebrate the life of Joseph McAllister. . . ."

It never once occurred to me that someday I might be sitting at Daddy's funeral. I never even thought about it happening when he was really old. I just never thought about it. Now I kind of wish I had, so that maybe I could be more ready for what is happening. But nothing could have prepared me for the death of the most important person in my life.

CHAPTER ELEVEN

One Year Later

I wake up with a stabbing pain in my side where Johnny tackled me. Every inch of me hurts. When I try to move, I have no strength to lift myself. My eyesight is blurry and one of my eyes is swollen shut. Because I can't see, I listen, to make sure Johnny is gone.

The wind in the trees sounds like the old widow-women gossiping in the back of the church. I hear the stream, too, rushing down the ridge, full of the autumn rains we had a week before. I cough. Pain fills my chest, and I taste dirt and blood. When I move my tongue over my teeth, I discover the rough edge of a front tooth chipped off. When I try to sit, I scream with pain and wonder if Johnny broke a bunch of my ribs. To my surprise, my scream doesn't sound like me, but more like that fox Daddy and I found in the woods once, its leg caught in a trap.

I yell for Mama, but the call for help sounds like a raspy whisper. I don't expect her to hear me, but more than anything at that moment I want a mother. Someone to hold me in her arms and tell me everything is going to be all right.

With my good eye I can see the sun is completely behind the mountain. It is getting dark. I must have been knocked out for at least an hour. My family will be looking for me now. Meg and Mama will know something is wrong. But how will they know to look on this side of the mountain?

The footbridge is just ahead. When Johnny caught me, I was halfway home and only a few steps away from getting free. If I can make it to the road somebody will find me. Otherwise I might have to stay here all night, and there will probably be a frost—or worse, Johnny might come back.

I struggle to pull myself up onto my hands and knees. My dress is ripped beyond repair, even by my sister, Amy. I do my best to cover myself but most of me is exposed. Without the sun it is much cooler. Every inch I move causes me yards of pain as I pull myself in the direction of the bridge.

I remember the dream I had where Daddy came to me. Was it really a dream? I call out his name now. But only silence answers me.

"I need your help, Daddy," I say, as I pull myself forward with all my strength.

I stop, hoping to hear his voice or revisit the dream. Tears sting my swollen eye and my nose drips from the tears. Another rush of pain shoots through me when I attempt to wipe my nose with my sleeve.

"My nose must be broken," I say to myself, "and maybe some ribs." Even though my voice is weak it feels good to hear it. It means I am still alive.

After I pull myself onto the first step of the bridge, I stop to rest. The one sturdy board I count on to get me safely across seems more narrow than it ever has. Not to mention that the broken hand-rail doesn't look stable enough to hold onto. My only hope is crawl-ing across, with the help of my one good eye.

More than anything, I want to go home. Mama will be mad at me for getting myself in this mess, but it doesn't matter. Nothing she can say or do will be worse than what I've already been through. I drag myself up the two rough steps and steady myself on the board. Then I shuffle my hands and knees forward. With every effort, I cry out in pain. What keeps me going is more than determination. It is anger. I refuse to let Johnny win.

The wind blows through the trees. For a second I think I hear Daddy's voice. I stop to listen. A squirrel chatters on a nearby tree. The bridge sways with my weight. I steady myself again and look up. Since this part of the handrail looks stable, I pull myself up to walk part of the way. I scream and cuss every bad word I know. I take the Lord's name in vain and then dare him to punish me for it. In the meantime, I hug the railing and sweat joins the blood on my face.

Now standing, I feel proud of myself and start to smile, but my busted lip won't let me. While clinging to the rail, I test to see if my feet will move. I take small, shuffling steps across the middle of the bridge. At a certain point I realize there is no turning back. The dan-ger behind is greater than what lies ahead. I call on every ounce of resilience I have and refuse to fall off the bridge into the ravine. I am like Mama. I will plow to the end of this row.

I reach for my medallion and then remember Johnny ripping it from my neck. I look back and think briefly about looking for it. But it is too much to ask myself to do. Instead, I pray for the good Mary's help and also help from the baby Jesus who we learned in Sunday school grew up to be a shepherd of people instead of sheep. Clinging to the rail, I pray to the Lord, who is my shepherd, not to ask me to lie down in green pastures just yet because I am not quite ready to go. I remember how Preacher read the 23rd Psalm at Daddy's funeral and had everybody say it with him. I have the opposite of still waters here, and my soul could use some help. And I figure I've already walked through the valley of the shadow of death and have seen evil right there in Johnny's eyes. I have trouble right now believing that the Lord is with me. I especially wonder where God was while Johnny was trying to knock my lights out forever.

When I reach into my dress pocket for my rabbit's foot from Woolworth's, I discover it isn't there. I sink my hand deeper into each pocket, thinking it must have fallen out while I ran. Without my medallion or my rabbit's foot I wonder if my luck has run out. I hold my head up and pretend the rabbit's foot is there anyway, as well as my Mary medallion. I give myself three wishes just to round things out. As I inch my way across the footbridge, I wish for courage, sure footing and strength. I thank the trees used to make the lumber to build this old bridge that holds me up. I thank the mountain for holding us all.

The board creaks from my weight and the sound of the stream grows louder. If I don't make it, people in Katy's Ridge will be telling the story forever about that unfortunate girl, Louisa May, who died one year to the day after her poor Daddy died in a horrible sawmill accident.

I take another step. A part of the board snaps. The bridge sways underneath me. A piece of bridge falls away, the size of a small cat, and my body goes rigid. That piece of bridge could have just as easily been me. It crashes on the rocks below. Dizziness sweeps over me as I try to steady myself. I cling to the rail, forcing myself not to look down.

The roaring stream calls out the danger below. After another step I see the end of the bridge and the path beyond. Pain stabs at me, and the tears won't stop. I push them back, thinking they will hinder my survival. My only job is to get back home where it is safe. I can't risk running into Johnny again.

"What did I do to deserve this?" I ask God.

As usual, he doesn't answer. What use is it to have a God who doesn't even help when you need him the most?

People aren't supposed to beat other people up. Johnny used me as a punching bag for all that had ever gone wrong in his life. Then he forced himself on me. That part I have trouble remembering. It's as if my mind wants to protect me from it somehow. But at least I fought back as much as I could. And even though Johnny nearly killed me, and threatened to finish the job if I told, I refuse to let him get away with this.

The handrail now gone, I drop to my knees and begin to crawl again. The board underneath me feels damp. A slippery smooth layer of moss covers the crevices. I grasp the dry edges and shuffle forward, an inchworm in human form. A steady, constant pain stabs at me with every move.

When I finally reach solid ground, I stay on my knees thanking God, Mary, the forest, and every rabbit that ever sacrificed a foot to bring good luck. Exhausted, I roll onto my side, wincing as I do. My cheek rests against the cold, moist earth. I wonder why life has to be so hard. It hurts to move. It hurts not to move. Nothing brings relief. I scream my frustration. My voice echoes faintly against the mountain. I scream again.

My head hurts so much I can barely lift it. Getting across that bridge was one of the hardest things I've ever done; now all I want to do is sleep. But I know how dangerous sleep can be. I need to stay awake, stay warm and yell for help. But when I try to stand the ground rolls and swells underneath me like a stormy ocean, and I begin to fall again. My legs buckle and the ground comes up to meet me. I hit hard. The fall knocks the last bit of fight out of me.

The earth is my bed; the rotting leaves my pillow. I want Daddy back. Preacher says God answers all our questions when we meet him face to face, and I have plenty of those. I want to know why he would let people like Johnny Monroe walk around just to hate and beat up other people.

Darkness is falling. It no longer matters if Johnny wins. All I want is rest. Life doesn't make sense. It doesn't matter if you're good or bad. People die for no reason. People suffer for no reason. I close my eyes and imagine my funeral. Silas Magee will make me a pine box, just like Daddy's but smaller. Miss Mildred will play something off-tune on the organ for me. Preacher will give me the benefit of heaven, since I've been baptized and accepted Jesus into my life. Mama might even cry, when she realizes how little she knew me. And I'll rest forever under the willow tree, right between Daddy and baby Beth, with a little marker paid for out of Aunt Sadie's quilt money reading *Wildflower McAllister, 1928-1941*. Like baby Beth, I will never age. I will always be thirteen. And then, every year on my birthday one of my sisters will wistfully say how old I'd be if Johnny Monroe hadn't killed me with his bare hands.

My body shivers and quakes from the cold. I wait to see what death will be like. Will it hurt? Will my soul throw off my body right in front of me?

In the distance, a light comes toward me. It is the most beautiful light I've ever seen—a combination of sunlight and moonlight, soft and rich, with gold, yellow and white rays coming out of the center. The gold Mary walks toward me with a lamb and a rabbit at her side. I am relieved to see the rabbit still has all his feet and luck with him. The gold Mary smiles at me and glows like the sun. Her rays wash over me, but don't cause pain, only strong, warm, peaceful feelings. The pain leaves me. I become the baby Jesus, resting in her arms.

I will join Daddy soon. We will rest in peace, watching the river flow by Katy's Ridge on its way to the Atlantic Ocean. In spirit, we'll flow with the river, making our way across America and across the wide sea to where my grandparents lived. We'll flow past my ancestors and up into heaven, making our way to God and Mary, where we'll never be alone again.

I close my eyes and let the ocean take me in her arms.

CHAPTER TWELVE

"There she is!" The voice breaks into my dream, sounding far away. I fight to stay where I am, to stay with the golden Mary. I am at peace. I'm not cold anymore.

I hear footsteps. I force one eye open and see a lantern swinging along the path. "Wildflower, is that you?" It sounds like Daniel's voice.

"Oh my God," Mama says in the distance. "What have you gotten yourself into now?" But I hear more fear in her voice than anger. It dawns on me that all her fussing my whole life has been about fear.

I feel regret that I won't be staying with the woman in gold. Her light disappears into the trees and the pain returns. Daniel and Mama arrive at my side. I try to turn in their direction but can't move.

Daniel wraps his jacket around me, covering my exposed skin. My eyes are swollen shut from my beating. The world is fuzzy and dark except for their voices. I listen as they discuss how to get me home.

"Hi Daniel," I say, as if we've just met on the road.

"Everything's going to be fine," he says to me. He sounds like Daddy for a second and tears come quickly to my swollen eyes. Salt water on a wound, the pain stabs fiercely to the point that I can't even scream.

"How bad is she?" Mama asks Daniel.

Daniel doesn't answer.

Mama holds the lantern close to my face. She gasps, as if not expecting what she sees.

"Let's get her home," she says to Daniel, her voice soft and sure. This attitude comes to Mama when a job needs to get done. This is the part of her I can count on. She will get me back home and patch me together again like a broken vase.

Darkness mingles with the lantern light as I sink into Daniel's chest and crawl inside his smell. A dreamy sleep carries me away. Daddy is carrying me now. He is still alive. He has been hiding in the woods. He was lost but now he is found, and he will never leave again.

Every few steps I am jarred awake. I am no longer a little girl and worry that I am too heavy for Daniel to carry. But he doesn't complain. In Daniel's arms, every inch of me cries out in pain. Mama doesn't speak but I hear her breathing next to Daniel's. They are moving as fast as they can without running. Mama pushes away tree branches and vines, clearing the path and telling Daniel the places to look out for, in that same strong voice she used when the men were bringing Daddy up the hill. I wonder if she knows something I don't know. Maybe I have that look that Daddy had, like I am leaving this world and there is nothing anybody can do to stop me.

Daniel's footsteps sound different when they reach the road. The earth has gravel mixed in it. The burden of carrying me runs up through his legs and arms and into me. We turn up the hill, and I know we are almost home. The earth is soft again. Mama's breathing is labored and so is Daniel's. They are racing up the hill in the dark. With one eye half open, I see stars and lantern light on a swatch of the hill. Daniel's chest heaves underneath my head, his heart and lungs calling on all their strength. I wish I was lighter so he wouldn't have to struggle. Maybe if I were light as a feather I could stay in Daniel's arms forever.

In the blurry, dreamlike darkness, Daniel smells just like Daddy—a mixture of sweat and sawdust, river and earth. I remember Daniel coming up the hill another time, the very first time he came to court Jo. He asked Jo out a few weeks after Daddy died, to go to a movie in Rocky Bluff. Jo had been so shy, which was really not like her, and she had invited him to dinner instead. He sat at the table where Daddy used to sit and Jo blushed more than I've ever seen her blush. Of course we all knew they'd get married after that. It seemed as sure as spring coming after winter, or the dogwood tree blooming down the road.

Preacher married them on a Sunday afternoon six weeks later and they went into Rocky Bluff for the night to have their honeymoon in a room at the Rocky Bluff Inn that Aunt Chloe and Uncle John paid for. It was like a fairy tale how much they loved each other. And now the king and queen are expecting a prince or princess.

Mama's footsteps reach the porch first. I am suddenly home free, as if I've been playing tag and have come to that safe place where no one can touch me. I love this porch. I love the steps, the floorboards, the railings and the porch swing that has hung there all these years.

"You're home, Wildflower," Daniel says, his breath still labored. But I hear relief in his voice, too. With the slam of the screen door the rest of the world goes dark.

CHAPTER THIRTEEN

"She's waking up," Jo says.

Hearing her voice, I wonder if I've fallen asleep on Daddy's grave again, and she's come to find me. Maybe I imagined the whole incident with Johnny Monroe and I still have time to get back to the house before Mama and Meg have time to worry.

I open the one eye that can still see. It is daylight again. Mama and Jo are there, along with Daniel and Amy. My face hurts like it is on fire. I touch my ribs and feel bandages wrapped around my waist, hoping Doc Lester wasn't the one who wrapped them.

I am laid out on Mama's bed like Daddy had been that last day. "Am I dying?" I ask softly.

"You're hurt pretty bad, but you'll mend," Mama says. She sounds confident and I believe her, though I've decided that dying might not be that bad. All your pain goes away and you get to see your loved ones again, not to mention the golden Mary.

"You need to tell us who did this to you," Daniel says, about as serious as I've ever heard him.

Everybody looks at me.

"You need to tell us," Jo repeats.

It isn't that I don't want to tell, I'm just afraid I'll be blamed for what Johnny did.

"You're not in trouble," Mama says to me, like she's been reading my mind.

"Whoever did this won't get away with it," Daniel says.

Amy is stone silent. This isn't that unusual, except she isn't looking at me. Her current silence has secrets in it, like she knows something I don't know. When I try to sit up, pellets of pain shoot through me like buckshot. I can't believe so many different places can hurt at once.

I am afraid to speak. Johnny threatened to kill me if I did. But I'm also too stubborn to let Johnny win.

"Tell us," Daniel says again.

I would do just about anything for Daniel after he carried me home in the dark. The look in his eyes tells me that it's okay to say it, that he'll keep me safe.

"It was Johnny Monroe," I say finally.

"I figured it was him," he says, looking over at Jo. "But we had to be sure. Nathan and his brothers are already out looking for him. His father said he hasn't been around for days."

Jo opens the curtains to let light in. I cover the one eye not swollen shut. I remember the golden Mary, her rays flowing straight through me. I look over at my family, wishing I could tell them about what I've seen. But they don't believe in ghosts or visions. Aunt Sadie is the only one I might tell—someday.

"The sheriff from Rocky Bluff needs to talk to you," Daniel says. "If you don't feel like it today we can put it off till tomorrow, but he needs to make a detailed report."

I can't imagine telling anybody all of what happened to me, especially a stranger. Not to mention that as soon as Johnny catches wind the sheriff is after him, he'll know I told. That's like putting a bulls-eye on my back.

"Maybe we don't need the sheriff," I say.

"Why not?" Daniel asks. It is the first time I've seen him even halfway angry.

"Johnny's probably long gone by now," I say, wishing my words could make it true.

"You can't let him get away with this," Amy blurts out. We all turn to look at her, the silent one in our family. "Well, she can't," she says.

I know she knows something. But whatever it is she won't say in front of the rest of the family.

"Did he threaten you?" Daniel asks me.

I don't answer.

"Don't believe it if he did," Daniel says. "He couldn't get to you now if he tried."

I am not so sure.

"Louisa May, you need to say what really happened," Mama says.

I am not so sure of that, either.

"You don't want Johnny doing this to anybody else, do you?" Jo says.

This much is true. I don't want anybody else getting hurt.

"The only place for Johnny Monroe is jail," Daniel says.

I pause. "Okay. I'll tell the sheriff," I say. My words come out mumbled from my busted lip.

"Good girl," Daniel says. "You just get well and we'll take care of it."

"What are you going to do?" Jo asks. She looks concerned. Like she's afraid Johnny might go after Daniel, too.

"Now that we know for sure, I'll go join up with Nathan," Daniel says to Jo.

Before he leaves the room, Daniel kisses me on the forehead and then kisses Jo lightly on the lips.

"How long have I been asleep?" I ask Jo, who is sitting next to me.

"Two days," she says.

"Two days?" I ask in disbelief. "I've never slept two days in my life."

"It's good for you," Mama says. "Doc Lester says you'll probably need to sleep for a week."

"You let that old horse doctor touch me?" I ask.

Mama and Jo smile at each other, like there is still hope if I am complaining about Doc Lester.

"He was the only one around to bandage you up," Mama says to me. "Sadie was out delivering a baby. She's over at the Sector's place now. June's having a rough time with her latest."

I remember the red gemstone Horatio Sector gave me the night Daddy died that is still wrapped in paper inside the leather pouch. I hope June is all right. And I am glad Doc Lester won't get a hold of her.

"Don't worry," Jo says. "Mama watched Doc real close so he wouldn't botch it up." Jo reaches over and holds my hand. "Do you need anything?" she asks.

"Maybe something to drink," I say. "My mouth feels like it's full of cotton."

"How about some sweet tea," Mama asks, as if happy to have something to do.

"Yes, please," I say, and it sounds like "yesh, peas." I touch my swollen jaw. Simply lifting my arm sends a searing reminder of what happened.

Mama leaves and Jo pets my hand while Amy sews. I've never known Amy not to be sewing on something. The world could be ending and she'd have a needle and thread, ready to stitch up a new one. Amy has also never been the type to dwell on bad news. Once things are done, they're done. But she is dwelling on something now because bad news is written all over her face.

Mama returns with the tea and I pull myself up in the bed, nearly screaming. Nothing has ever been this hard for me. All these years, I took feeling good for granted.

"Just try to stay still," Mama says, with the tone of voice she used when I was a little girl acting up in church.

Jo shoots her a look like Mama needs to behave. I've never seen Jo defiant, especially to Mama, but even in my pain I enjoy it. "What would make you more comfortable?" Jo asks me.

"Can you help me sit up?" I say.

Jo helps me sit upright against the pillow even as I yelp and moan. I sip the tea slowly, taking in the liquid on the side of my mouth that doesn't hurt.

"Are you hungry?" Mama asks. She doesn't take to sitting still.

"A little bit," I say.

"I have some leftover cornbread," she says. "Would you like that?"

"That sounds good," I say, grateful that there is still something so ordinary and perfect in the world as Mama's cornbread. "Maybe I'll talk to the sheriff tomorrow," I say to Jo. Every word I utter is through gritted teeth, to keep my face from hurting.

"I'll tell Daniel," she says.

Lying there, it's impossible to take in all that has happened. I want my old life back. I want to be an innocent, thirteen-year-old girl again. Too much has changed. I survived the wrath of Johnny Monroe, but just barely. How do I know he won't come looking for me again? Maybe I shouldn't have been so quick to tell who did it.

Mama shows up with a large piece of cornbread on a plate. Jo breaks off tiny pieces and puts it in my mouth like I am a little bird in a nest waiting for its mother to bring a worm. The cornbread, cold and a day old, is still delicious. I yawn, which causes excruciating pain, and I can't believe how sleepy I am even though I've already slept for two days.

With Jo's help I take bird-sized sips of tea and listen to my family talk about normal things. In a way, this is a salve that soothes me most. My family speaks about what needs to be done to get ready for winter and about Jo and Daniel's baby that will be coming next spring. We are awash in normalness, but I can't help noticing that nobody is talking about what happened to me.

I drift off to sleep again and when I wake up the house is dark and quiet. For the longest time I lie motionless in the dark, trying to guess what time it is. Going by the stillness, I decide it must be the middle of the night. I fold my arms across my chest like Daddy when he was laid out in this same spot. I hold my breath, pretending I'm dead, with mourners all around me. I imagine the gold Mary coming to get me, letting me ride in her golden arms to heaven where Daddy waits for me. Then it occurs to me that maybe the gold Mary came for Daddy, too, and that he went to that place that was peaceful and warm. The thought of it makes me want to cry with happiness and sadness all at the same time.

I inhale deeply and my breath catches like barbed wire in my chest. I cuss under my breath, going from heaven to hell in one second. Cussing is a sin, according to Preacher, but it has its place with this level of agony.

Despite the pain, my body wants to function naturally. I need to go to the bathroom. When I notice a figure near the wall, I jump and wince with the pain of moving too fast. My immediate thought is that Johnny has come back to finish the job he started. But then I realize it is Mama, asleep in her rocking chair in the corner. It surprises me that she has stayed so close. "Mama?"

She startles awake. "Joseph?"

"No, Mama, it's me," I answer. "Louisa May." I haven't called myself by my regular name in four years. But it feels like the part of me that was "Wildflower" died in the woods.

"Louisa May, what is it?" she says. She stands in the shadows. With her hair down she could easily be one of my sisters.

"I need to pee," I say.

"I'll go get Bessie," she says, the name for our chamber pot. Daddy was always naming things, like the stand of four red bud trees at the bottom of the hill that Daddy named as sisters, all starting with the letter "S." Sally, Susie, Shirley, and Samantha Red Bud.

"I don't want Bessie," I say. "I need fresh air. I've been in this stuffy old house for days."

Mama doesn't argue. "Do you think you can walk?"

"I don't know, but I might as well find out," I say.

She helps me out of the bed and holds my arm as I shuffle through the living room and into the kitchen. I move at a turtle's pace. With every step it feels like Johnny still has a hold on me, squeezing the breath out of me. My head throbs. I feel sick to my stomach. The pain has worn me out, like a dishrag squeezed dry.

With Mama's help, I slide into a pair of Daddy's boots at the back door that we all use when we go out back in the middle of the night. As a little girl I always liked the feel of my small feet clomping around in his big old boots. At thirteen, they are still roomy, but not nearly as much.

We cross the back porch and Mama lights a lantern to help us make out the steps. With a full bladder, the path to the outhouse seems unending. The October air has turned cold. We arrive at the privy with the half-moon Daddy carved in front. The door creaks open and then slaps closed. The smell of lye and earth and urine hits my nostrils. The half-moon lets in a whisper of fresh air, and I aim my nose in that direction. Mama stands outside with the lantern. My pee lets loose, and I feel instant relief. But the pee burns as it comes out, which doesn't feel right. I've never burned down there before.

"Mama, something's wrong," I say through the door.

"What do you mean?" she asks.

I can hear her shuffling her feet like she is cold.

"My pee burns," I say.

Her silence answers me. I don't know what it means that she isn't saying anything and now I'm sorry I even brought it up. When

I come out of the outhouse she has the light pointing down the path toward the house and I can't see her eyes.

"Damn that Johnny Monroe," she says. "I hope he rots in hell."

I've never heard Mama damn anybody before, but then her anger turns toward me. "Louisa May, you don't have the sense God gave you. What were you thinking going out to that graveyard on your own like that?"

Shame crawls up the base of my spine. Did I somehow give Johnny permission to do what he did? My mind flashes on Johnny unbuckling his pants, but I erase the image as quickly as it comes.

"I was just visiting Daddy's grave on the one year anniversary," I say in my defense.

Mama stops mid-stride, as if she's just realized it's been a year.

"There's no use crying over spilt milk," Mama says, the words rough as burlap.

Our breath races toward the moonlight. There is a frost tonight. A hoot owl cries out in the night.

Mama holds the lantern closer to my face, and I cover my eyes to avoid its glare.

"We need to go inside," she says. "It's cold out here."

We walk back to the house in silence. I make the same slow shuffle as when we came out. It irritates me that I want to run and can barely walk. Yet what hurts me more than anything Johnny could do to me is Mama's silence. Her judgment sinks into me like a heavy stone thrown into the river, its ripples extending out from me for maybe years. She blames me for getting hurt. If I had stayed at home that day and forgotten Daddy, just like her, nothing would have happened.

Silent as Daddy's grave, she helps me back into bed.

"Try to get some sleep," she says, pulling the blanket over me.

Before she turns out the light I get a full dose of the disappointment in her eyes. Besides beating me within an inch of my life, Johnny has stolen something from me that I might never get back: Mama's respect.

CHAPTER FOURTEEN

The next morning Sheriff Thompson of Rocky Bluff knocks on the door. When he enters the room I determine that he is the biggest man I've ever seen. The gun strapped around his waist looks small in comparison to the rest of his body. Though he towers over everyone in the room, he stoops his shoulders as if trying not to be so big. In spite of his size he seems kind enough, replying "yes, ma'am" to Mama when she asks him if he wants iced tea. Iced tea runs as free as well water around here. Mama leaves the room to fill his request. Aunt Sadie arrives shortly afterwards with the news of the Sector's new healthy baby boy. She sits on the bed next to me. I don't care how old I am, having Sadie nearby always makes me feel braver.

"Your name is Louisa May McAllister?" the sheriff asks.

"Yes," I answer.

My name had been Wildflower, but I don't feel like Wildflower anymore, not wild or beautiful in any way. Johnny's laughter echoes in my head. *Wildflower? People should call you weed . . . I think I'll pull this weed.*

Sheriff Thompson clumsily juggles a note pad and the glass of tea Mama hands him and places the glass on a quilt square on her dresser. "I need to know what happened between you and Mister Monroe," he says.

I've never heard anybody call Johnny *Mister Monroe.* It sounds unnatural. Johnny hasn't earned the "Mister" yet. As far as I'm concerned, he never will.

"He came up behind me at the graveyard," I say, my words still coming out in mumbles.

"Graveyard?"

Aunt Sadie sits next to me like a rock, her only job to be solid. She wraps her warm hand around mine and encourages me to go on. I wonder how she and Mama could be so different.

"I was visiting somebody," I say. "It was the anniversary."

"Anniversary?"

I feel irritated. If the sheriff is just going to repeat everything I say this is going to take forever.

"Of when her father died," Sadie says.

The sheriff taps the side of his note pad with his pencil like he is putting something together in his mind. "What time of day was it?" he asks, "when Mister Monroe came up behind you."

"Early afternoon," I say.

I don't tell him that the secret sense told me I shouldn't go and how I ignored it. I haven't told Aunt Sadie, either. I don't think I could bear her being disappointed in me, as well as Mama.

"And what exactly happened when Mister Monroe came across you in the graveyard?" he asks, his pencil poised to take down my answer.

With all this time in bed, I've had a lot of time to think. I figure I've grown up in these last few days. I can't look at the world in the same way anymore. Truth is, things happen that you have no control over and sometimes people act in ways that make no sense. From now on I'll be watching over my shoulder to see who might be coming.

"Like I said, Sheriff, Johnny came up behind me in the graveyard. And when I tried to get away he grabbed my wrist, and I couldn't get free. Then I hit him really hard in the nose and made a run for it. I took the shortcut I found, because I thought that would get me home the fastest, and that maybe Johnny didn't know that back way as good as me."

I sit straighter with Sadie's help. My head has ached for days and all these questions are making it worse. Though the pain has lost its ragged edge, I am still reminded of what happened every time I move.

The sheriff takes a sip of tea and wipes the droplets off the dresser top with his sleeve. "Please go on," he says, sounding more official than he looks. Dark hairs grow out of his nostrils and join up with his mustache. From this angle I also see that his socks don't match, though his shoes are as shiny as Doc Lester's hearse the day of Daddy's funeral.

"Well, Johnny caught up with me," I say. "I bit his hand pretty bad when he tried to cover my mouth."

"Why did he cover your mouth?"

"Because I was screaming bloody murder!"

"Wouldn't you?" Aunt Sadie says to the sheriff, putting a protective arm around me. He gives her a long look, clears his throat and looks at his notes.

"At what point did Mister Monroe leave?" he asks me.

I want the sheriff to quit calling Johnny *Mister* Monroe.

"I don't know," I say. "I passed out and when I woke up Johnny was gone. After that, I knew my family would be looking for me, so I started trying to get home."

The screen door squeaks open, slams, and Daniel walks in. He and the sheriff greet one other. Then the sheriff turns his attention back to me.

"I suppose that wasn't easy," the sheriff says, "hurting as you were."

"No sir, it wasn't," I say.

I can only imagine what the sheriff sees when he looks at me. A thirteen year old girl with two black eyes, a swollen jaw and bruises on her throat and arms that are deep shades of red and purple and yellow, like the fabric Preacher slung over the arms of the cross at church during Easter. I don't see any reason for the sheriff to know everything, at least not now and maybe never, so I stop there.

"Is that all?" the sheriff asks.

I consider for about a half a second telling him about Johnny messing with me. That is the real crime. But with my family all around me, I don't have the guts to say it. Not to mention that Sheriff Thompson is a stranger. Mountain people don't trust strangers, even if they only live over the next hill. "That's all," I say.

"One more question, Louisa May. Do you know the direction Mister Monroe went in after he left you?" he asks.

I pause to remember any clues in those last seconds before Daddy came to get me. I can't think of anything else so I shake my head, no.

"I don't think he would have crossed over that bridge," Daniel says. "I got a look at it the other day. A girl could cross it, but not a man. He must have backtracked to the graveyard or went higher up on the ridge. Those Monroes know these woods pretty good."

"Were you the one who found her?" the sheriff asks Daniel.

"Yes. Me and Nell, Louisa May's mother."

Daniel looks over at me like he's caught himself not using my real name. I don't know how to tell him that it doesn't matter anymore.

"When we found her she was pretty bad off," Daniel adds.

"You're lucky you found her," the sheriff says. "We've had cases that don't turn out that well."

It is hard to imagine anything really bad happening around Rocky Bluff. Maybe a shoplifter gets caught at Woolworth's or somebody accidentally shoots themselves in the foot while cleaning their shotgun.

Sheriff Thompson closes his note pad. "Well, we'll get men out looking for him," the sheriff says. "Don't worry, Louisa May. If he's still around, we'll get him. But chances are he's long gone."

I like the thought of Johnny being long gone, but I doubt I could be that lucky. Johnny can hide out in the woods for years if he wants to and once he finds out that I told what happened, he'll want revenge.

"So you don't think he'll come back here?" Mama asks.

"No ma'am. I don't think he will," the sheriff says.

"He wouldn't be that stupid," Daniel says.

But Johnny is that stupid, I think. *He'll come back to kill me just like he said he would.*

Daniel leaves with the sheriff, and I hear them talking as they go down the hill. Aunt Sadie opens her cloth bag and puts a gooey yellow salve on my cuts and bruises that smells like beeswax. Her touch is gentle. Mama is in the kitchen again, clanging pots and pans, getting supper ready. Since the night before she's hardly spoken to me. When Sadie finishes, I am sticky and fragrant and wouldn't be surprised if a colony of bees came searching for me, their new queen.

Later in the afternoon Amy comes to sit with me so Aunt Sadie can go back and check on June Sector. This is the first time since Amy's odd behavior the day before that I've had a chance to talk with her. She leans against the back of the bed next to me, a pile of fabric in front of her. Of all my sisters, Amy and I are the most distant. I wouldn't dream of telling her my secrets because she's never told me hers. She also hasn't once mentioned Daddy since he died. It's like her feelings are all sewed up inside her, without an inch of give in the fabric.

I wonder how to get her to open up when she speaks first. "I was in the same year as Johnny in school," she says.

"Yeah, I remember," I say.

She sews a few stitches while I wait for her to go on. When she doesn't continue, I think I'll go crazy from the waiting.

"He used to say mean things to me," she says finally. "At least until Nathan came along."

It never occurred to me that Johnny might have spread his meanness around to Amy before it landed on me.

She keeps sewing like she hasn't said a thing, and I feel the gate she's just opened starting to close. But I am not willing to let it. I prop myself straighter in bed so I can be eye-level with her. "Amy, what did Johnny say to you?"

She pauses, as if she's remembering every single word. "Things I wouldn't want to repeat," she says softly. She stops sewing but doesn't take her eyes from the fabric. "Once he pushed me down on the ground while nobody was looking. You have to understand, Louisa May, I thought it was just me," she adds. A tear falls into the folds of the fabric.

"Why didn't you tell anybody?" I ask, sounding too much like Mama.

She returns to her sewing, making quick, jabbing strokes. "I did tell somebody," she says. "I told Nathan, because Nathan and I were friends. After we started courting he told Johnny if he ever said anything else to me he would kill him. Johnny left me alone after that. It never occurred to me that he would--"

Amy puts her head in her hands and bursts into tears. Since I've only seen her cry once, right after Daddy died, her tears feel like something wild and dangerous that might swallow her up.

"It's okay, Amy," I say. I touch her hand, wanting to release her from whatever she is holding against herself.

"Maybe if I'd said something this wouldn't have happened to you," Amy says, still sobbing. She looks miserable.

"Even if you'd told the whole world it doesn't mean Johnny would have done anything different," I say.

Her gratitude shows in her face. "I'm so sorry, Louisa May." Amy blows her nose on her handkerchief.

"What about Jo and Meg? Do you think he said anything to them?" I ask her.

"I think he left Jo alone. She's older than him, and you know Jo. She's so beautiful. I don't think he had the nerve. But I don't know about Meg."

"Meg told me once to stay away from him," I say. "That he was a no-good. But I didn't ask her what she meant."

For the first time since she arrived, Amy puts down her sewing and looks at me. She looks like Mama, but younger, and without looking cross. "I'm really sorry this happened to you," she says, her eyes red from the tears.

"It's not your fault," I say.

"But it is," she says. "Johnny started saying those things to me right after Daddy passed. I should have told Mama."

"But you didn't want to worry her," I say. "I didn't tell her what Johnny was saying to me on the road because I was afraid she'd think I did something wrong."

"I guess you do understand," Amy says.

"Somehow Daddy dying gave Johnny open season on us McAllister girls," I say.

Amy looks thoughtful. "I think you're right, Louisa May. "He never bothered me before that." She continues her sewing and I am struck by the fact that this is the most we've ever confided in each other.

Later that evening, with Mama and Meg in the kitchen, I quit fighting the memories and let them come. I open my nightgown and study my wounds. The bruises on my body are evidence not only of a beating but that Johnny messed with me, too. The bruises on my inner thighs and breasts look like hand prints. Doc Lester must have seen them when he bandaged me, as well as Mama. Maybe even Jo saw them. But nobody is talking about it.

CHAPTER FIFTEEN

Like a friend who goes away because you never listen to them, my secret sense seems to have left me, too. I sleep uneasily that night. Every time I roll over I am reminded of my bruised ribs. I listen to the house settle into itself, creaking with the slight breeze. I have my ear trained outside, listening to every little sound in the woods, afraid Johnny will come looking for me. Several times a night, I'm convinced I hear someone walking up the path to the house and get out of bed to make sure the doors are locked.

The next day the house is empty except for Mama, who is on the back porch beating the dust out of the rugs with her broom. The wallops echo through the house. She beats them with such force I wonder if she is imagining Johnny Monroe as one of those rugs. Or maybe me.

Holding my bandaged ribs, I shuffle into the living room in my stocking feet, crossing the patches of sunlight making tree shadows across the wooden floors. The metal of Daddy's banjo splinters light across the ceiling. I take the banjo from its place, then sit in the rocker and hold it for a long time, my nose right up next to the wood. I search for reminders of Daddy's scent, but all I can smell is Mama's lemon oil. I touch the strings he touched, imagining that their tautness helps me hold myself together.

I hug the banjo so hard it starts to dig into me. For a second the pain in my chest takes my mind off the pain in my heart. But then the memories return. They always return. A gentle breeze in the yard reminds me of the sound of the wind in the trees that day. The smell of dust and dirt from Mama's rugs causes tightness in my throat and the feeling of Johnny's hands pressing on my windpipe. Vivid details spring to life. I remember the buttons on Ruby Monroe's dress as she hung in the oak tree watching me. And the look in Johnny's eyes as he crouched on top of me like an animal cornering his prey.

Careful not to nick the wood, I put the banjo back in its place. I haven't told anybody about Daddy appearing to me. It seems too crazy. But he had been there for me, as real as anything. Just like Ruby had been there to witness the scene.

A huge lump of anger wedges in my throat. I resent that Johnny will always be a part of my history now. I can try to forget the beating, but the rest I don't think I can forget. He got what he wanted all along. I was just a stupid girl who thought nothing bad would dare touch her again after she lost her father. But I figure bad luck, like good luck, never gets used up.

As for God, I no longer know what to do with him. Since I was *washed in the blood of the lamb* at eight, as Preacher says, it looks like God could have at least warned me, or protected me from Johnny. After Daddy died, I'd pictured them both up in heaven watching out for me. Daddy sat at God's side, telling him about his Wildflower here on earth. But now, it feels like both have disappeared. Cuts and bruised ribs can heal. But how do you get over heaven turning its back on you?

Becky Blackstone comes over that Saturday to work with me on my schoolwork so I won't get too far behind. I have missed the beginning of the school year. She is the new teacher at Katy's Ridge grade school. It feels weird to call Becky, *Miss* Blackstone, and obey her every word because she is only four years older than me. She graduated high school early and went to two years of teachers college. When she was a student at the Katy Ridge School, Becky always acted like she was better than everybody else and talked real big about getting out of Katy's Ridge someday. So we were surprised that she came back. Her father owns the sawmill and was Daddy's boss. When we were younger, Becky never let me forget that fact. But she seems different now.

Becky makes herself at home in Mama's rocker, wearing a dress that has a flower print with a lace collar. At that moment, she seems younger than me, chewing on the eraser of her pencil and quizzing me on my history lesson. It makes no sense to study world history when I have my own more recent history to deal with. I've aged in the last few days. I've seen and felt things I hope other girls never have to at thirteen, or at any age.

Mary Jane comes to visit only once, just after the attack. She says her mother doesn't want her to disturb me. But I think her mother is just afraid that some of my bad luck might rub off on Mary Jane. Mary Jane acts like she, too, wonders what I did wrong, and what I could have done to prevent it. For the first time in our long friendship there are silences that I don't know if we can get beyond.

By way of Meg, Victor sends over three packs of peppermint lifesavers from the store. I pocket them to have handy when I can't sleep in the middle of the night. It is just like Victor to do something sweet like that.

That afternoon, after Becky leaves, Preacher's booming voice greets Mama at the door. He comes into the bedroom and walks over next to me. He reeks of mothballs, church hymnals and sweat.

"I trust you're doing well, Louisa May," he says, his Sunday morning voice too loud for the small room.

I sigh, sorry to put down the book I've been reading. Boredom has set in and Preacher isn't helping. He crosses his arms across his chest, Bible still in hand, and looks at me over his glasses. He visits shut-ins and sinners and I'm not sure which camp I fall into.

"Let's see what I can offer you today," he says. He thumbs through the worn leather Bible and reads out loud for several minutes about people being blessed for being meek and lowly. I think "cursed" might have been closer to the truth. Meek and lowly wouldn't have saved me from Johnny. If I'd acted meek and lowly I'd probably be dead.

By the time he finishes reading he has lambs lying down with lions, which doesn't make sense given my life lately, either. I don't have the energy to question him. The quickest way to get rid of him, I decide, is to nod my head every now and again and say, "Amen," until he's convinced his words have sunk straight into my soul. That way, Preacher will think he's delivered God's message loud and clear and I'll be rid of him.

The next day is Sunday and Mama and Meg go about the business of getting ready for church.

"Jo and Daniel are coming over later to visit while we're gone," Mama says. "Do you need anything?" she adds, tightening the bun of her hair. I like that she is doting on me a little.

I pull myself up in bed. "I'm fine," I say. It's not really true but I know it's what Mama wants to hear.

She takes off her apron and folds it neatly before she puts it on the dresser. Church is about the only place she goes without her apron on, except for maybe a rare trip into Rocky Bluff. She straightens the covers on the bed, pulling the corners so tight I can't move my feet.

"That hair of yours is a mess," she says, taking a closer look at me. "I'm surprised mice haven't made a nest in those tangles."

"I'll comb it later," I say, a lamb to her lion.

I roll over and close my eyes, pretending to sleep. I listen as Mama and Meg chat while they finish getting ready for church. They have an ease with each other I envy.

Jo calls hello from the front porch and the screen door squeaks before slamming in the familiar way. It never occurs to us to grease the hinges. That was Daddy's job.

I hear Daniel's voice, too, and I wonder if he's heard any news from the sheriff. They talk softly in the living room at first, so I scoot out of bed, put a blanket around my shoulders and shuffle toward their voices. I hide behind the door. I can't see but I can hear them pretty well.

"They think he's done this to other girls, too," Daniel says, his voice low. "There's at least two in Rocky Bluff that say somebody attacked them in the woods near there."

"Poor Louisa May," Jo whispers. "I can hardly stand to look at her with all those bruises."

"That's the price you pay for taking shortcuts through the woods," Mama whispers back.

"Oh, Mama," Jo says, "why are you so hard on her?"

Silence answers. I start to wonder if eavesdropping is that smart a practice since a person might accidentally hear something they don't want to hear.

"She's just so much like your father," Mama whispers finally. "It's like being haunted by a ghost."

Mama's voice breaks. She excuses herself and I hear her go into the kitchen. I hobble back toward the bed just as Jo comes in.

"What are you doing out of bed?" Jo asks.

"I'm tired of just laying here," I say, hoping she doesn't realize I heard.

"You must feel better, then," Daniel says, entering the room behind her. "I'm not one to lie around either."

"You want to play a game of checkers?" Jo asks. I can't remember the last time she asked to play checkers. Maybe never, but I pass.

I ask Daniel if he's heard anything from the sheriff and he says no.

"We'll be back soon," Mama calls from the front door. She and Meg leave, and Jo and Daniel and I go out on the porch to sit in the sun. It is chilly, but not cold, and the blanket is warm around my shoulders. In mid-October almost all the leaves are off the trees, but it is still warm in the middle of the day. So warm you can almost trick yourself into thinking that spring waits just around the corner instead of winter.

While I lean against the porch post, Jo rests a hand on her newly bulging stomach. Daniel sits on the step below me, whittling a piece of wood. I remember the cat he made me for my birthday, a day that now feels in the distant past, even though it was just two weeks ago.

"You really do look like you're feeling better," Jo says.

"A little," I say.

"You know, you gave us quite a scare," she says.

"I know." I wrap the blanket closer, thinking about how I haunt Mama just by being alive.

Jo leans toward me and smoothes my hair. I lean into her touch. At that moment, I feel like a little girl and a grown woman at the same time, a frequent occurrence these days.

"I know just what you need," Daniel turns around and says to me. He winks at Jo. "Let's go down by the river."

My body tightens with fear. The river is one of my favorite places, but I don't want to go.

"I don't know if I can walk that far," I say. I've been holed up in the house long enough to see the value in it. Walls keep a person safe. Locked doors do, too.

"I don't think I've ever heard you turn down a trip to the river," Daniel says. He glances at Jo, like maybe he's stopped worrying about me too soon.

I think about it for a solid minute and weigh all the things that could go wrong—meaning Johnny—and how wonderful it would feel to visit a place so beautiful. "I guess we could try it," I say finally.

We go inside and Jo goes into my dresser drawer to get a sweater for me to wear and helps me pull it over my head. I make sounds like I'm being tortured. Then she helps me pull on an old pair of pants. My boots, next to the door, are scrubbed clean, as if Mama took her strongest bristle brush to them.

We walk slowly down the hill and I remember the last time I traveled this path in Daniel's arms. My heart beats faster than usual and my eyes dart left and right. I realize I am looking for Johnny behind every tree and rock.

"What's the matter?" Jo asks.

"I'm having a hard time breathing," I say.

Daniel and Jo stop and turn to look at me.

"We're in no rush," Daniel says. "Just take your time."

"But what if he's watching us?" I say to Daniel. My voice sounds small.

"Johnny's probably a hundred miles from here by now," Daniel says. "Sheriff seems to think he's long gone, too. He'd be an idiot to stick around here after what he's done."

I want to believe him, I really do. We start walking again and Daniel and Jo each offer a hand for me to hold onto. After we travel down the road a ways, it starts to feel good to be out of the house. The air is crisp, but not enough to show your breath, and the sun warms my back. I could have done without the sweater, but don't want the pain of taking it off.

We pass the twisted dogwood that hides my shortcut to the graveyard. It isn't a secret anymore, and Daniel takes a long look as we pass as if he's remembering that night, too.

With the baby coming, Jo and Daniel seem happier than ever. They act like newlyweds, giving each other glances that are full of secret meaning. If Meg saw this, she'd be swooning all over the place.

I haven't taken the path to the river since the day of Daddy's accident, afraid it would remind me of all the sadness. But when we get closer I realize how much I've missed it. The path narrows as me and Daniel and Jo walk single file through the reeds. Daddy and I always held our fishing lines over our heads through here, so that our lines wouldn't get tangled. The river gurgles its greeting, ripples expanding outward from the shore.

At the riverbank, Jo spreads a blanket she's brought and we sit; Daniel on one side, Jo on the other. We watch the water for a long time, as if settling into its rhythms. It is a perfect day, blue skies and sunny. I throw a pebble into the water and watch new ripples break the glassy surface.

Daniel weaves two grasses together and places it in my hand like he's offering me a gift. Then his face turns serious, as if he's been waiting for this moment to tell me something.

"Johnny Monroe had no right," he says softly. "You need to know that."

"But Daniel, I shouldn't have gone out that day," I say. "It's my fault."

"You have the right to go anywhere you want, Wildflower," he says.

"You don't have to call me that anymore," I say.

"What do you mean? That's your name," Daniel says.

"It sounds silly, now," I say, ready to be Louisa May the rest of my life.

"But it's the name Daddy gave you," Jo says.

"I know. But nobody has a name like that," I say.

"Don't let Johnny do this to you," Daniel says. "You can't let him take away your name or your freedom. You're the same person you were."

"No, I'm not," I say. The words feel as true as anything I've ever spoken. "I wish I were the same person, Daniel, but I'm not. That girl, Wildflower, died that day," I add. "She was innocent and naïve and stupid."

"Don't say that," Jo says, looking me squarely in the eyes.

"That's what Mama thinks," I say. "Not to mention, I haunt her because I'm like Daddy."

Jo and Daniel exchange looks.

"Your mama isn't herself these days," Daniel says. "But that's not the point. I don't care what anybody says, you haven't done a damn thing that was wrong."

I pause, grateful for Daniel's words, and hope someday that I believe them.

"I just wish it had never happened," I say finally. "I knew I shouldn't have gone, but I did it anyway."

"We all do things like that," Jo says. "We all have regrets."

I can't imagine Jo regretting anything, but I let it go, like the stick I throw into the river that rides out of sight on the current. After that, we watch the river for a long time. Then a question rises to the surface like one of the trout in the stream. I take this as a good sign since lately I've been more full of fear than questions.

"Why do you think bad things happen to some people but not to others?" I ask. "Mary Jane hasn't had a single bad thing happen to her in her whole life and probably never will."

"Damned if I know," Daniel says. The wisdom of his statement makes me smile, but Jo doesn't seem to see the humor in it.

"We've just got to trust that God knows what he's doing," Jo says.

Without Jo seeing, I roll my eyes toward heaven, which I'm not so sure exists anymore.

Jo takes a good look at the bruises healing on my face. "Does it still hurt?" she asks.

"Sometimes," I say. What I don't tell her is that the memories hurt more than all these physical things combined.

Since yesterday I've been able to see out of my left eye again, and the bruises have changed from red to purple edged in yellow.

The three of us rest on the riverbank letting the sunshine warm us. The church bell rings in the distance, the service over. Coming here feels more like church than Preacher reading from a book and telling us what sinners we are.

"Thanks for bringing me out here," I say. "I'm glad we came."

They each give me a hug and afterwards we retrace our steps back to the house. I didn't lie to Daniel. A part of me did die that night. Despite my belief, I repeat to myself Daniel's words: *You haven't done a damn thing that was wrong.* For the first time in days, I feel myself starting to get better. I also feel something new. I feel mad. Really mad. More than ever, I want Johnny Monroe to pay.

CHAPTER SIXTEEN

For two weeks I slept in Mama and Daddy's bed while Mama slept in mine. This was special for a while, but now it feels good to get back to sharing a room with Meg. We are both in our nightgowns and getting ready to turn out the light.

"Are you really going back to school tomorrow?" Meg asks.

"I've got to go back sometime," I say.

"Things have probably died down by now," she says. "But there will probably be some whispering."

I'd like to think everything could get back to the way things used to be, but that feels like childish wishful thinking. Lately my stomach has been hurting, too, but not enough to tell anybody. Aunt Sadie is away for the day collecting her remedies and I don't want Mama calling Doc Lester. As long as I have feet instead of hooves, I don't want him near me. At least the bruises have faded and I'm sleeping through the night again without waking up and worrying about Johnny hiding in the woods. But I still spend a big part of my day wondering where he is and if he will come after me again.

The next morning I get ready for school like nothing has changed. Mama makes oatmeal with molasses in it and wraps me up a meatloaf sandwich to take for lunch. Daddy used to say that Mama's meatloaf sandwiches would give a condemned man something to look forward to. That always made Mama smile. But I am not about to mention it now. I don't want to haunt Mama anymore than I have to.

Meg caught her ride with Mr. Appleby earlier that morning, and when I reach the bottom of the hill Jo and Amy are waiting to walk me to school. In the last weeks, my sisters have gathered around me like guards surrounding the British crown jewels that Daddy read us a story about when we were younger.

When I walk through the doors at school, all eyes are on me. Mary Jane is already there and her face lights up like it is Christmas and the 4th of July all at once.

"I'm so glad you're back," Mary Jane says.

I sit at my desk. "I'm glad to be back, too," I say, which is partly true. For some reason, school doesn't seem as important as it did before.

"You act different," Mary Jane says at lunchtime.

"I feel different," I say.

We trade half of her egg salad sandwich for half of my meatloaf one. She is definitely getting the better end of the deal. The Bronson brothers, Kyle and Mark, look at me and whisper. I pull on my dress wondering what they've heard.

I feel sick at my stomach again. While Mary Jane and I eat in silence, she looks at me like I've become a stranger. In a way, I have.

Two weeks pass and my appetite doesn't return. Mama makes my favorite, chicken and dumplings, convinced I need to get some meat back on my bones. Our chickens are in a pen to the side of the house, near the old shed, so the foxes can't get to them. They have a coop where Mama collects eggs from the hens. She wrings their necks with one, quick whip. Even though fish guts don't bother me, killing chickens is something I can't bear to do, and luckily she doesn't make me.

Nobody has seen Johnny in weeks and his family has deserted him. According to the Katy's Ridge grapevine, Arthur Monroe has left Katy's Ridge to stay at the Veterans Hospital in Nashville and Melody went to live with an aunt in Louisville, Kentucky, where she has a chance at a better life. Meanwhile, I cling to the belief that Johnny is long gone like Daniel and Sheriff Thompson think.

The next day after school, Daniel meets me to walk over to Aunt Sadie's to get some chamomile tea to settle my stomach. Max runs down the road to meet us. He barks until he recognizes us and then wags his tail in wide circles. Max's eyesight isn't that good anymore so he relies mostly on scent. His hair has turned gray like an old man's. Sadie serves him up one of her potions every night, mixed with supper scraps, which probably keeps him alive longer than most dogs his age.

Aunt Sadie waves when she sees us. She is preparing her garden for the cold weather to come. Winter knocks hard on the door of Katy's Ridge, but today has been warm, inviting people outside to get a few things done. I have not minded winter so much this year. If Johnny is hiding in the mountains, I want him to have every opportunity to freeze to death.

Sadie stands and hugs us both. She studies me, looking deep into my eyes, as if I am a patient of hers that requires a diagnosis.

"I was just going to put on some cider," she says. "Would you like some?"

I say, yes, but Daniel says he has to get back to Jo. He hugs Aunt Sadie and says his goodbyes. "I'll be back for you in an hour or so," he says to me.

I nod, grateful that he is so protective of me.

After Daniel leaves, Sadie gives me another hug like I could use an extra dose. Then we go into the kitchen where she serves me a mug of cider. She makes apple cider with secret ingredients in it that she promises to pass on to me someday. With mugs in hand, we go back and sit on her porch swing. Then we take sips of the warm brew.

Max claims a worn spot in the flowerbed below us. His panting looks like a wide smile. Sadie doesn't scold him out of her flowerbeds anymore since he's good about staying in the one spot.

I sit quietly, something I do a lot these days. I want to confide in Sadie but ponder the words I might use. Meanwhile, Sadie studies me like I am a storm forming over the mountains. We take turns swinging the porch swing with one foot, letting the squeaking metal serenade us. It sounds like the crows in Nathan's fields calling to each other after the crop is in. Their squawking conversations are loud enough to hurt your ears.

The wind picks up. I pull my frayed coat closer to my neck, buttoning the top button that Mama replaced the night before. I am always losing the top buttons of things, just like Daddy.

"If you're cold we can go inside," Aunt Sadie says.

"I am a little bit, but I like it out here," I say.

The squawking metal hooks announce what I'm about to say.

"Aunt Sadie, if I talk to you about something will you promise not to tell anyone? Especially not Mama."

"Of course, honey," Sadie says. She takes my hand and squeezes her promise into it.

I pause. "My insides don't feel right," I say finally.

"Describe to me what you mean," she says, her face as serious as any doctor's.

"My stomach feels queasy a lot, except for no reason. It's not like I've been sneaking pieces of Mama's pies or anything."

We sip apple cider. Its secret ingredients help settle my stomach. Sadie nods like she's consulting the dictionary of ailments stored in her memory and then stops the swing.

"Are you still having your monthlies?" she asks.

I think back to the last time I washed out the cloth pads Mama made me. It was my birthday, a good six weeks before. "No," I say.

I don't like the expression on her face, which reveals both concern and sadness.

"What is it?" I ask.

"It could just be the trauma," she says.

"The trauma?" I don't even know what a trauma is, but it doesn't sound good. To see Sadie so serious worries me.

"I know we haven't talked very much about that day," Sadie says.

"Nobody has," I say.

"Well, that's not a good thing," she says. "I guess we haven't known what to say. What happened to you was just so horrible, honey." She pats my knee, as if she remembers every bruise. "But still that's no excuse." She pauses. The blue-gray of the sky is mirrored in her eyes. "Country people gossip like blue jays when something happens to somebody else, but when it hits close to home they don't know how to talk about it. I knew that, and I did it myself."

"It's okay," I say. "I haven't known how to talk about it either."

"Honey, I need to ask you a very hard question," Sadie says.

I don't like hard questions and feel queasy again, but I tell her to go ahead and ask.

"Did Johnny do anything to you that you haven't told us?"

"What do you mean?" I ask, but I know exactly what she's referring to.

Max comes up on the porch and puts his paws on my lap.

"Good boy, Max," says Sadie. "He always knows when he might be needed." We pet him and he takes up his new nap place near my feet.

I think the worst: that because Johnny messed with me I'll be joining Daddy in the graveyard after all because Johnny has given me some disease that kills people.

Sadie stops the swing and turns to face me. "Did Johnny take advantage of you, honey?"

Tears rush like a flash flood down my cheeks, leaving no room to turn back. Aunt Sadie squeezes me tight. The dam in my memory bursts open and I tell her everything. I tell her about how I told Mama I was going to the river but I really went to the graveyard. And how the secret sense told me not to go but I ignored it. Then I tell her about how Johnny was there at the graveyard and how he spit tobacco juice all over Daddy's grave marker. I tell her about running for my life and almost making it to the footbridge but then Johnny catching me instead. I tell her about him beating the living daylights out of me and then taking Grandma McAllister's necklace. Then I tell her about what else he did to me that I swore I would never tell another soul. At this point, Sadie is crying, too. Big tears that slide down her cheeks and collect like raindrops on her shoulders.

"Johnny called me Ruby when he was messing with me," I say. "He cussed at me for killing myself. What he did to me must have been the same things he always did to her. That's why she killed herself, Aunt Sadie. Johnny hurt her, too."

Sadie listens to me as if hearing me out is the most important thing she might ever do.

"And the baby Ruby carried to her grave, Aunt Sadie, it must have been Johnny's. It had to be."

Sadie holds me firm, like an injured bird that might flitter away. She rocks me in her arms while the truth settles in. A bright red and orange horizon settles behind the ridge. I begin to cry like I cried at the river the day Daddy died. I didn't think I'd ever cry like that again. But I do. I cry for Ruby. I cry for the girl I used to be. I cry for all the girls that have ever been made to do things against their will. And I cry for the baby that possibly rests below my heart.

After I empty myself of tears, I feel almost relieved, like some poison has been released from a wound. Sadie dries my face with a clean handkerchief and gives it to me to blow my nose.

"What am I going to do?" I ask, searching her face for answers.

"We need to wait another month to make sure," Sadie replies. "Then if it's true, we'll just deal with it."

"But what about Mama?" I say. "She'll kill me."

Of all the people that might find out, I dread her the most. But hasn't she suspected it already?

"Your Mama's survived worse, so don't you worry about her," Aunt Sadie says.

Max barks, announcing Daniel coming back to pick me up. He's in his old truck now and I'm glad we don't have to walk home. I blow my nose one last time on Sadie's handkerchief. Daniel won't mind if I cry, but I just can't bear to tell him yet.

"Let me give you something for the nausea," she says. Sadie walks to the opposite end of the porch where her herbs are planted. She takes a handful of leaves and crushes them between her fingers and puts them in a small paper bag. "Chew on these whenever you feel it coming on. I'll bring you more later." Then she goes to her cupboard and pulls out a jar of blackberry wine for me to give to Daniel in exchange for bringing me and picking me up.

Before I leave, Sadie hugs me so tight I can hardly breathe, but it feels good. Daniel waves from the end of the road and waits for me there.

"Don't count your chickens before they're hatched," she says to me. "We've got a few more weeks before we know for sure."

"It's our secret, right? At least for now?" I ask.

"To the grave, if that's how you want it," she says.

I trust Sadie to keep that promise.

When I meet up with Daniel, I pretend that everything is fine. I am getting good at pretending. Max walks with us to the end of the road and then turns back. On the way home, I wonder if Daddy took any secrets to the grave. I guess everybody has them. I picture the graveyard full of secrets, tidy little packages tied onto the limbs of the weeping willow tree.

CHAPTER SEVENTEEN

Whispering in the kitchen wakes me up early. I usually sleep later on Saturdays if Mama will let me. But the air is full of secrets that are as tangible as the smell of coffee. The last time there was whispering in the kitchen was after Ruby Monroe died. I get out of bed and follow the voices to the kitchen. Mama and Aunt Sadie are talking with Daniel and Nathan.

"What's going on?" I ask, wiping sleep from my eyes. It is the first day I can walk without pain or soreness.

"She needs to know," Daniel says to Mama, using his full voice.

Nathan agrees, and then hitches up his pants. Everybody looks at me and the urgency of their looks makes me shiver like someone just walked over my grave.

"Somebody better say something soon," I say.

Mama flashes me an irritated look. "We found a note on the porch this morning," she says.

"From who?" I say, but I've already guessed.

"Johnny," Daniel says, confirming my fears.

The queasiness in my stomach moves up to my throat. "How do you know it was Johnny?" I ask.

"Well, we don't know for sure," Nathan says.

"What did the note say?" I ask. I want to know, but at the same time I don't.

Nathan hands me the note written on a crumpled, dirty piece of brown paper bag. In childlike handwriting it says: YOU TOLD. YOUR DEAD.

Daniel is right. The note has to be from Johnny.

"Where was it?" I say. I take on the manner of a detective and don't let on how terrified I am.

"Under a rock on the front stoop," Nathan says. "I guess he snuck up here in the middle of the night."

The thought of Johnny Monroe only a wall away from where I slept gets my body to shaking. Aunt Sadie puts a protective arm around me. She squeezes my shoulder while Mama sits at the kitchen table. Mama looks tired, like I've made one too many messes that she has to clean up.

My bladder sends an urgent message. "I've got to go up the hill," I say. *Up the hill* means the outhouse. Daniel follows me out and keeps an eye on the woods.

I follow the stone steps, imagining Johnny's invisible footprints are all over the place. A potent morning pee splashes dully into the dirt below the sitting hole, giving me time to think. Like everybody else, I wanted to believe that Johnny was gone and that nothing more would come of him.

When I return to the house the whole family sits around the kitchen table and Mama has biscuits just out of the oven. Her biscuits can cure just about anything, but I still have a gnawing feeling in my stomach that no food is going to help.

"I think Max should stay up here with you all for a while," Aunt Sadie says. "He won't let anybody get within fifty feet of the house without barking."

Mama likes dogs even less than she likes cats, but she puts up with Max because of Sadie.

"Max is a good idea," Daniel says, "but I think we need to do more than that. We've got to find Johnny."

Nathan nods and swallows a mouthful of biscuit. "If Johnny's in these mountains somewhere, he's got to come down before the snows come," he says. "Unless he's in a cave somewhere, but even then he'll need to get his hands on some warm clothes."

"We need to call the sheriff and tell him what's happened," Daniel says, "and then I think we need to go looking for Johnny ourselves."

"Can I go with you to make the phone call?" I ask Daniel. He'll have to make the call from Mary Jane's and I could use a friend right now. But the main reason is I want to stay close to Daniel. I feel safe with him.

"Sure," he says.

"From now on you're not to go anywhere alone," Mama says.

"At least not until Johnny's caught," Daniel agrees.

We walk to Mary Jane's and Daniel calls the sheriff while Nathan waits on the front porch like he is a sentry standing guard. Nathan's grandfather fought in the Civil War for the Confederacy and died at the battle of Vicksburg. Nathan's family still has the sword he carried in the Calvary.

Even though it has been nearly a hundred years ago, people in Katy's Ridge still talk about the war like it has just been fought. Daddy always said that people in the South have long memories. With this in mind, I wonder how long it will take me to forget Johnny.

"I can't believe he left a note," Mary Jane says. "And right on the front porch."

"It was creepy," I say. We sit on the bed in her bedroom. If feels like a hundred years since we did this last.

"Are you scared?" she asks.

"Sure, I'm scared. I'd be stupid not to be." Even though Mary Jane is trying to be nice, I realize she has no idea what this is like for me.

"Johnny wouldn't have the nerve to do anything else," she says. She chews on the ends of her hair.

"Yes, he would," I say. "If anybody knows first hand what Johnny Monroe has the nerve to do, it's me."

Mary Jane gets quiet. Ever since Johnny attacked me, she seems different. Or maybe I am the one who is different. Mary Jane still daydreams about boys and about having a fairy tale wedding some-day. All I think about is how to stay alive in this moment.

"Are you ready to go?" Daniel says to me after he makes the call. In Mary Jane's bedroom, his head nearly touches the top of the door-frame.

I get up from the bed and take one last look around the room as if I am trying to remember my childhood. Everything has changed. Everything.

"Come over later if you want to do something fun," Mary Jane says.

Playfulness feels like something I lost at the footbridge, along with my medallion, my rabbit's foot and the secret sense.

"It'll probably work better if you come over to my house," I say. "And have Victor walk you so you don't have to go alone."

She frowns, like being my friend isn't any fun anymore and comes at too big of a cost.

Daniel and Nathan and I walk the dirt road back to the house, and I remember all those walks I took in the evenings with Daddy. Back then it never even entered my mind to be scared of anything, or that there were bad people in the world who might be watching.

"One of us should be at the house all the time," Daniel says to Nathan.

Nathan agrees and says he'll take the first shift. Later that night, he sleeps on the sofa while Amy sews in the kitchen. I come in to get a glass of milk and Amy is working on Miss Mildred's latest dress request, a direct copy from the Sears & Roebuck catalog. Daddy's shotgun sits next to the kitchen table, loaded, a package of shells sitting next to it. She sees me looking at the gun.

"Don't worry, Louisa May, they'll get him," Amy says. Her long hair is in a loose braid.

I always thought me and Amy were as different as night and day. But Johnny threw her to the ground, too, though she never said he did any more than that. Knowing Johnny, he must have tried. But how did Amy escape and not me? My brain is too full of fear to ask.

After drinking the milk, I say my goodnights and go to the bedroom where Meg is already snoring like a lumberjack. She always falls asleep before me. Instead of the porch, where Max usually sleeps, he lies on the floor next to the bed, close enough that I can lean down and pet him.

"Thanks for being here, Max," I whisper, "and don't you worry about Sadie, she'll be just fine." His tail dusts the wooden floor.

It takes forever for me to fall asleep and then when I finally do, a loud gunshot, in the middle of the night, shakes us all awake. Meg and I run in the direction of the shot, following Max who is barking like crazy. Mama, Nathan, Meg and I all arrive in the kitchen at the same time.

The back door stands wide open. Amy has Daddy's shotgun still aimed at the door. Her arms are shaking and the gun rattles with the movement. The acrid smell of gunpowder fills the room. Max runs outside and continues barking on the back porch. Nathan takes the gun from Amy.

"I think I hit him," she says, her voice quivering. "He jimmied the lock and came right on in. I didn't even have time to call out or anything. But he didn't expect I'd be sitting here waiting on him."

Amy buries her head in Nathan's chest, her entire body shaking. "I think I hit him," she says again, her words muffled in Nathan's shirt. She's crying now.

"Go get Daniel," Mama tells Nathan, stepping in to hold Amy.

Nathan does as he is told and goes into the living room to lace up his boots. Within seconds he runs out the door with a lantern. Through the living room window I watch the light he carries fade and then disappear down the hill.

As Meg reloads the shotgun, I pace the house. A kitchen chair is jammed under the doorknob in case Johnny returns. Amy is still shaking like a leaf in a strong wind. But after I tell her about our watchdog, Max, not waking up until the shot, she starts to laugh.

"Max slept through it?" Amy asks. "So much for him not letting anybody get within fifty feet."

"He was curled up in our room," I say.

Amy's laughter calms her and she stops shaking.

"Don't tell Sadie," Mama says. "She thinks that old dog can walk on water."

"Well, at least he's doing a good job, now," I say.

Max hasn't stopped barking on the back porch, no matter how much we try to shush him. Maybe his old man pride is injured and he's trying to make it up to us.

Mama passes Amy to Meg and puts on a pot of coffee while we wait on the men to return. I sit in Daddy's chair in the shadows of the living room, wishing he were here. My hands are shaking now and before I have time to stop it, vomit rises in my throat. I rush outside and heave over the porch rail into the dark night. It is as if my body wants to rid itself of all the fear. The purging feels awful and good at the same time.

I hear Meg's voice behind me. "Are you okay?" she asks.

"Not really," I say truthfully, wiping my mouth on my night-gown.

"We should tell Mama," she says.

"No," I say. "Definitely not."

"Why not? If you're sick she needs to know."

"I'm not sick, I'm just scared," I say. *And maybe in a family way,* I want to add.

The first hints of daylight outline the mountains in front of us. I turn around. Meg looks worried.

"I'm okay," I say to reassure her.

Seconds later we hear voices. It is Nathan, with Daniel and Jo, coming up the hill. Nathan and Daniel carry shotguns.

As soon as the sun comes up more and they are full of Mama's coffee, Daniel and Nathan go out back to search for clues.

Daniel calls from halfway up the slope that he's found blood.

"Amy must have hit him!" Nathan calls back. He sounds proud.

It never occurred to me that Amy might be a good shot. Daddy taught us all how to shoot, but none of us have ever really practiced. Amy must have a good eye from all that sewing.

The men come back into the house to warm themselves by the stove and plan what to do next. Mama pours them more hot coffee.

"If he's hit we may be able to catch him," Daniel says.

"I agree," Nathan says, "and we need to leave soon if we're going."

Nathan hitches up his pants and tightens his belt while Mama wraps up some ham and biscuits for Daniel to pack in his day bag. They grab their shotguns by the door and are about to set out.

"Wait a minute. I want to go, too," I say. They turn to look at me and I pull myself up to my full height. "If anyone is going to hunt down Johnny Monroe, it's me."

"No you aren't," Mama says.

"I don't see any harm--" I begin.

The look on Mama's face is designed to shut me down.

"I'm not a little girl anymore, Mama," I say. "It's important that I do this. In fact, it may very well be the most important thing I ever do."

My words make me feel strong again, like I may be Wildflower McAllister after all.

"Daddy would understand this," I continue. "You see, Mama, I can't let Johnny Monroe win. If I do, I will forever be looking over my shoulder for him to come back and finish what he started."

"But you're still on the mend," Mama says.

"I feel fine," I say. "Nothing hurts anymore."

Daniel and Nathan stay quiet, as if they know better than to get between Mama and an argument. Mama looks at me for a long time, like she's seeing the ghost of Daddy again and is just now realizing how much she misses him. To my surprise, she nods her okay. Before she has time to change her mind, I give her a quick hug and grab one of her biscuits and wrap it up in a rag.

Within seconds, Nathan leads the way up the hill. It's steep and I'm grateful my soreness is gone. Daniel and Nathan stop to look at something on a cropping of rocks. Daniel motions for me to come look. A blotch of red blood is splattered on the gray stone.

"He's been hit, all right," Daniel says.

"Where do you think he's going?" I ask.

"Probably back to where he's been staying," Daniel says.

For the rest of the morning we wander the mountainside like Indian trackers, searching for which way Johnny might have gone. At the top of the ridge we come to a waterfall that I've only been to once before. Daddy brought me up here a few years ago to show me one of his favorite places. I was still small enough to ride on his shoulders.

The water plunges dramatically over the mountain and down the gorge. The spray from the waterfall chills my face. In the middle of winter icicles edge the rocks. Rosettes are frozen into the mud, paw prints of a big cat, either a wildcat or maybe a cougar. We study them for awhile before continuing on.

Nathan knows this part of woods better than Daniel and I do. He motions for us to follow him as he seeks out the best place to cross. The closer we come to the waterfall the louder it roars. Mist, churned up from the pounding of water, covers our faces. My teeth chatter from the cold and I pull my wool jacket closer. When I reach to button the top button, it isn't there.

The Farmer's Almanac predicts this winter will be worse than normal. On a normal year we average a foot of snow in December, January, and February. But Thanksgiving is still two weeks away.

We cross several large boulders and come to a place where the water calms. I recognize the place. It is near where Daddy and I found the red fox in the trap.

Nathan points to where we will cross. The sight of the ravine makes my heart pound like the day Johnny chased me.

"Don't worry," Daniel says, putting his arm on my shoulder, his habit with me. "It's not as bad as it looks."

"I hope not," I say. We have to speak loudly to be heard over the waterfall. A thick pine tree leans into the waterfall several feet downstream offering a limb to grab if I need it. The footbridge I cross to get to the graveyard is nothing compared to this.

"Hold onto me," Nathan calls. He hoists up his pants one last time, and I grab his belt. He leads the way with Daniel following me. They put their two shotguns on either side of me like handrails that I can hold onto while we cross. The metal of the guns is ice cold, even through my gloves.

Nathan tests out each step before committing to it and makes his way slowly across the slippery rocks. As soon as his foot leaves a spot I put mine in the same place. The roaring of the waterfall pushes us forward.

I slip and bite my lip and taste my own blood. My vision whirls as the taste of blood brings back the memory of Johnny hitting me in the face. I start to fall and Daniel grabs me from behind.

"Careful there!" he says. He pulls me up by the seat of my pants and places me back on the rock like I weigh no more than a sack of potatoes. My heartbeat echoes in my ears and drowns out the sound of the waterfall. We make our way across boulders as big as a house to get to the other side.

"How are we doing back there?" Nathan asks, not turning around. We are halfway across.

"I'm doing fine," I call over the roar of the water, wondering how I've become such a good liar.

"We're almost there," Daniel says. "We've already done the hardest part."

I remember my words to Mama earlier and wonder where that strong girl went who had the gumption to convince her I could do this. If I had the sense to stay home, I could be sitting in front of the stove having one of Mama's biscuits right now.

When we step on solid ground instead of boulders, I am not the only one relieved. We sit on a dry boulder and Nathan wipes the mist from his forehead. Daniel pats him on the back like he did a good job in leading us. Nathan, always hungry, pulls shelled walnuts out of a pouch for us to eat. They taste good but smell musty, like they have been in that pouch a long time.

"Everything's downhill from here," Daniel says to me.

"Do you really think Johnny came this way?" I ask.

"He might know a better way across," Nathan says. "His daddy had him up here hunting as soon as he could carry a shotgun."

I can't imagine Johnny ever being a little boy. The thought of him rushing to keep up with his father makes him seem too human. I know him as almost a man, and mean.

After we rest we make our way down the other side of the mountain. We don't find much of anything in the way of clues. Squirrels dash to unbury nuts they've stored for winter, making enough noise for us to look to see if it is Johnny.

Our footsteps are loud in the brittle leaves. If Johnny were anywhere around he'd be able to hear us coming, and it makes sense that we could hear him, too. Anytime we stop the forest hushes. Below us, in the distance, is the old footbridge. It looks tiny from this position, a splinter of toothpick, barely in view even with the leaves off the trees.

We descend the mountain and reach the path and the clearing where Johnny caught me. Goose flesh crawls up my arms and I shiver with the feeling that I've just walked over the very spot where I could have died. In my memory the area had grown larger than what I find before me, which is little more than the size of the pitchers mound at school. A fresh blanket of autumn leaves covers the ground. The browns and golds mingle with the forest undergrowth. Dying fern fronds wave at us in the wind. A piece of my dress from that day is hanging from a pale spire of a broken flower. I retrieve the piece of red fabric and put it in my pocket.

"I was hoping we'd catch up with him by now," Nathan says.

"Did you think he doubled back?" Daniel asks, as he leans on the barrel of his shotgun.

"I doubt it," Nathan says.

I leave them talking and sweep the leaves away with my boot looking for my medallion. I've been afraid to see this place again;

afraid the memories would chase me back home. But being here, I realize that it is just a place in the woods. It is not the forest that is dangerous. It's Johnny.

In order to stay there longer, I remind myself that I didn't die. Johnny didn't kill me. He wanted to. He meant to. But he didn't. If God and I were still on speaking terms, I'd ask him if he has some special plan for me, like Preacher said about Little Wiley Johnson, who swallowed half the lake, spit it back out and lived.

While Daniel and Nathan stand near the old bridge in a patch of sunlight, I push more leaves aside with my boot and see something white peeking from underneath. It is my rabbit's foot key chain. I hope this means my luck has changed. I pocket the rabbit's foot, wanting to find my medallion, too. I'd worn that medallion around my neck for an entire year. To have Johnny take it added insult to my injury. Especially after I had that vision of the gold Mary walking toward me in the forest.

Before I give up and walk over to Daniel and Nathan, I spend several minutes looking around, turning leaves over with my foot.

"I didn't know this path was here until the other day," Daniel says to Nathan.

"I think it used to be part of an old Indian trail leading to the river," Nathan says. "This old bridge is useless now, though."

I don't mention how many times I've managed to cross that useless bridge to get to the graveyard. I reach into my pocket and squeeze my rabbit's foot thanking it for the good luck it has sent me in the past.

"We should head back," Daniel says. "I'm meeting the sheriff later."

Nathan hitches up his pants. "He needs to get some hounds up here. That's the only way we'll find him."

While I wait, they discuss what to tell the sheriff and I realize how tired and cold I am. Being back at the scene of Johnny's crime reminds me too much of what happened. My determination, so bright before, turns into dull exhaustion. I sit on one of the wooden steps to the bridge and gaze at the distant stream, making its way down the mountain toward the sea.

All of a sudden, something shiny winks at me from the bottom of the ravine. It is a tiny glimmer of light, like the sun reflecting off the silver of Daddy's banjo in the living room. The wind blows and the sunlight makes its way through the trees from directly overhead. I lose sight of the flicker for a moment, but then see it again. Raccoons steal shiny things, but it doesn't look like an area where raccoons would nest. I stand to get a better view and step closer to the edge. I train my eyes to make out familiar shapes. Amid scattered sunlight and shadows, the glimmer of light continues.

"What is it?" Daniel asks.

"There's something down there," I say. "But I can't make it out."

Daniel stares where I point. Then Nathan comes over and does the same. The light flickers again and they both see it this time.

"Let's go down there," Nathan says.

"You think that old bridge can hold us?" Daniel asks. He doesn't look like he's so sure.

Nathan studies it for a while. "If we do it right," he says.

One by one we cross the rickety wooden bridge. I go first and squeeze my rabbit's foot and long for my medallion. Because I still hold a grudge, I don't pray to God and his angels like I would have done before. But I thank the bridge for holding us up and keeping us safe. Halfway across I notice a section of the bridge is missing. I take short, careful steps around the missing section. If there is a baby inside me, I want to keep it safe, even though a part of me hates it for even existing.

Daniel and Nathan follow. They cross, stepping lightly and fast like they are dancing over a hot fire. If they are scared they don't show it. And it is the one time Nathan doesn't stop to hitch up his pants.

Once we are on the other side Daniel leads the way. We leave the path and go down the hillside toward the ravine. The steepness of the rocks makes it slow going. My legs ache from all the walking and climbing we've been doing and I'm still tired and cold. After about 100 yards, Daniel stops and looks over at Nathan. Then he points to something up ahead that I can't see.

"Is that a deer carcass?" Nathan asks Daniel.

"I don't think so," Daniel says. They exchange another look.

"Maybe you should go back and wait for us at home," Daniel says to me.

"I don't want to," I say bluntly. I am tired of being treated like a child.

"I don't want your mama mad at me," Daniel says.

"Not a chance," I say. "She thinks you're the best thing since electricity."

Nathan chuckles.

"Come on, then," Daniel says to me.

I smile, having won a small victory for my independence and follow them into the gully of the ravine. As we walk, I catch glimpses of what is ahead, but I can't clearly see until we stop at the edge of the stream. What Nathan thought was a deer, is a crumpled body in a brown coat. A pool of dark red blood covers the rocks around the body.

Nathan makes his way across several boulders to get a better look. "It's Johnny!" he calls.

I gasp.

"Wait here," Daniel says to me.

I start to follow anyway but he holds out a stiff arm to stop me. His look convinces me I should stay.

Daniel and Nathan turn Johnny over.

Johnny is dead. His skull is cracked open and there is a ragged wound in his thigh from where Amy shot him.

"He probably tried to cross that bridge with the frost still on it," Daniel says.

As if wanting to protect me from the sight, Daniel takes off one of his flannel shirts to put over Johnny's head. Before he covers Johnny's face he leans down and takes something from around Johnny's neck. Then he walks over to me.

"This must have been what you saw from up there," he says.

Daniel hands me my medallion of Mary with Johnny's blood crusted over the baby Jesus. I wash it off in the ice cold water of the stream. The fear and anger I've felt since Johnny attacked me, washes away with the blood. I take a deep breath. For the first time in weeks I feel safe.

I don't know where Johnny will end up for eternity. But in a twinge of mercy, that surprises me, I hope he finally gets to see his mother again and his sister Ruby. I hate Johnny for what he did to me. Like Ruby, it seems he's already lived a life close to what I imagine hell to be. Maybe God will take that into account. If God exists after all.

CHAPTER EIGHTEEN

After the hard winter the Almanac promised, spring shows off in a big way. The first buds are on the trees and the weeping willow has feathery, light green leaves on the tips of its limbs. Sitting in the graveyard, I feel different now. I spent the whole winter holed up in the house. Some days it was so cold we kept our gloves and scarves on all day and didn't venture far from the wood stove. But we survived.

The air still has a hint of coolness to it, like the last little bits of winter are blowing through. Warm breezes promise to follow—breezes filled with the heavy summer sweetness of blossoms and ripe fruit.

Sitting next to Daddy's headstone, I rub my swelling belly that holds Johnny's baby inside. For months I hated this baby, just like I hated its father. But my hatred wore itself out over the long winter and I decided not to blame the baby for being there. Just like me, it had no choice in the matter. But in the middle of the night when doubts creep in, I still blame myself and I think Mama blames me, too.

A week before Christmas, Doc Lester showed up at the house to talk to me about ways to get rid of it. I knew Mama had put him up to it and I cussed them both to their faces before I made Doc Lester leave. After that, a silence settled between Mama and me that feels permanent.

At least my sisters and Aunt Sadie haven't deserted me. Amy, as quiet as ever, has never spoken again about Johnny. But she comes over and sits with me and sews me new clothes big enough for my swelling belly. She also stitches little outfits for the baby, both pink and blue. Over the winter, Meg took to reading me romance novels out loud. I was so bored, I let her.

Jo is due any day. But I can't help but wonder if some of the joy has been robbed from her because of me. People can't look at her without thinking about me. The two McAllister sisters, both with child, one by good fortune and one by misfortune—the white and the black sheep of Katy's Ridge.

I'm not sure I'll ever get used to the whispers in church. Preacher doesn't come by anymore. Nothing in his big black book instructs him on what to do with an unwed mother whose child was conceived the way mine was. In my own way, I have become Mary Magdalene. It doesn't matter that in the Bible story Jesus was nice to her and considered her a friend in the end. Niceness is too much to ask of the self-righteous of Katy's Ridge.

I don't go to school anymore and do my studies at home. Becky Blackstone comes over every Saturday and ignores the growing lump under my clothes week after week. After about a month, I started calling her Becky again, instead of Miss Blackstone, and she doesn't seem to mind.

Mary Jane's mother won't let her come over anymore. If we see each other at the store or on the road, Mary Jane acts strange, like she doesn't know what to say to me. Her brother, Victor, is the only one who acts like nothing has changed. When I go to the grocery for Mama he always asks how I am and he smoothes his hair down to look nice. This makes no sense given my new role as outcast. But I appreciate the gesture. Probably more than he will ever know.

Horatio and June Sector invite me over for a picnic in their backyard the first warm day of spring. The kids are all running around barefooted, though there's still a chill in the air. I am beached on a faded old quilt and I don't think I could get up on my own if I had to. Their new baby, about six months old now, is asleep on the edge of the quilt. We fish pickled eggs out of a jar and have honey on fresh baked bread, the pure goodness of which gives me hope that life might be normal again someday.

Horatio is dark golden and has blue eyes. His wife is just the opposite. June is light skinned and blond headed but with dark eyes that seem to penetrate right into your soul. I show Horatio the ruby he gave me which I have started carrying in the same pocket as my rabbit's foot.

"That's a star ruby, Miss Wildflower, and very rare."

No matter how many times I ask him not to, he always calls me "Wildflower." I thank him again for the ruby.

"I still miss your pa," Horatio says.

"I still miss him, too," I say.

"A spring day as beautiful as this is for the living, not the dead," June says. She is always direct. A trait that is as rare as a star ruby here in the South.

June feels around on my stomach like she's counting fingers and toes through my skin. "It's a girl," she says, "on account of how you're carrying."

Something about hearing that makes having a baby seem more real. Over the winter, I spent a good deal of time pretending it wasn't happening at all, in spite of the fact that it was getting next to impossible to tie my shoes. Now I just wear old sneakers with the laces out of them.

"This baby is going to be good for you," June tells me. "Don't you listen if people tell you different. She's going to grow up to be very important. A prophet of some kind. Just like you are."

Besides being a mama to four kids, June is also a fortune teller and I wonder if she is reading my future and can see the secret sense there. Maybe I haven't lost it forever after all. Something about the beauty of the day and the possibility of good coming out of the badness of Johnny Monroe makes me smile.

Horatio and June are outcasts, too, and I make up my mind, then and there, that being in exile from all the people on the mountain that make judgments may be a good thing.

The next week I go spend time with Aunt Sadie. Her house is about the only place I feel at home right now. But even Aunt Sadie is sad these days because Max died on Christmas eve. Daniel and Nathan helped bury him out behind her house. Nothing could console her losing her best friend, so even Christmas was a sad day this year.

I feel like I've lost my best friend, too. Not just Mary Jane, but Daddy. When I sit in the graveyard now, it's like he's finally gone. We don't have conversations anymore, and I can't hear what he's telling me. Under the ground is nothing but a box of bones, a skeleton of memories. The fleshy parts, things I thought I'd never forget, are fading and turning to dust.

"I'm sorry if you're disappointed in me, Daddy," I say, looking at the sky in case he's up there now. The willow tree brushes its leaves against me in the breeze.

I lower my gaze and notice someone walking up the hill toward me. At first I think it might be Johnny and my whole body stiffens and I get ready to run. But then I remember that Johnny is dead and in an unmarked grave next to his sister Ruby.

Once I get the old memories out of the way, I smile when I see who it is.

"I thought you'd be here," Daniel says. He tosses a piece of straw onto the ground that he's been chewing.

I brush leaves aside so he can sit next to me. "Don't you have anything better to do on a Saturday?" I ask.

"I could ask you the same," he says. "But Jo wanted me to check up on you."

"Mama used to be the one who'd send someone, but I guess she's given up on keeping track of me," I say.

"Give her time," Daniel says.

I feel like I've given her enough time. She's been different ever since Daddy died, and even before that she was not all that patient with me. Now with the baby growing inside me, I've given up hope that we'll ever be close again.

Daniel and I sit together and look at the river in the distance. A whooping crane walks the edge of the reeds. It's one of a pair of cranes who spend spring and summer in Katy's Ridge. I don't see its mate.

"How's Jo?" I ask.

"She's good," he says. "About to bust like an overripe melon," he adds, smiling.

I smile back at him, but then grow serious.

"Daniel, things are so messed up," I say. "You and Jo haven't been able to enjoy your baby coming as much because of me."

"It's not your fault," he says. "We all go through hard times."

"But why do things like this happen?" I ask. This is just the kind of question I would have asked Daddy to ask God for me. But God and I have not been on speaking terms for months now.

"Wildflower, I have no idea," he says.

"Please don't call me that," I say, patting the roundness of my stomach. The girl I used to be has been buried in an unmarked grave, too.

"I like the name Wildflower," he says. "I think it's about time you claimed it back."

"My name is Louisa May," I say. "Plain and simple."

I glance at the newest mound in the graveyard, a lump of red dirt next to Ruby's pile of weeds and dirt. I think of Johnny's crumbled body at the bottom of the ravine, wearing my medallion. As far as I know, he didn't even have a funeral.

"There's nothing plain and simple about you," Daniel says.

We settle into silence. As hard as I wish it never happened, I can't wish this baby away. It would be like trying to wish away the river in front of us. This baby will have a hard enough life without a mother who wished she'd never been born. The gossip in Katy's Ridge will follow her around her whole life. To be a bastard child is just about the worst thing you can be around here, other than colored or Indian.

"What do I do now?" I ask Daniel, resting an arm on my belly.

He pauses like this question requires thought. "No matter what life delivers to us, I think it's important to live with as much honor as possible," Daniel says.

"That sounds just like something Daddy would say," I tell him.

He smiles like I've given him a huge compliment. "Just remember you're not alone. We're all in this together."

"Tell Mama that," I say.

"She'll come around," he says, like he believes it.

"But I'm not so sure I want her to come around," I say. I never told Daniel about Mama bringing Doc Lester to the house to tell me ways to get rid of the baby. If he knew, he probably wouldn't forgive her, either. "I watched a bird once," I continue. "It was pushing its baby from the nest. The little bird fought back, but the mother bird was bigger and pushed it out. The little bird had a bad wing and fell to the ground. It didn't get up again." I pause. "That's Mama, Daniel. I'm on my own, whether I have a bad wing or not."

He nods like he's heard me, but doesn't necessarily agree.

I trace the dates on Daddy's tombstone with my finger, following a familiar path. "This October will mark two years since he died," I say.

"Has it been that long?" Daniel asks.

"Too long," I say.

Daniel looks out over the river. "I can see why you like to come up here," Daniel says. "It's beautiful."

Ducks honk as they fly overhead and skim the water below in perfect landings. It wasn't the beauty that drew me here in the past, but the feeling that Daddy was here. Now he seems as silent as Mama.

"Are you ready to go home?" he asks.

"I'd like to go to Sadie's instead," I say. "I think she's lonely since Max died."

"I'll walk you there," he says.

The walk is long since I don't take the shortcut anymore. On days like this I wish we had a car. Daniel and Jo have their old truck but it only works half the time. Despite my complaining, it is a lovely day and it feels good to stretch my legs.

When we arrive at Sadie's house she is sitting in a straight-back chair on the porch, a butter churn between her knees. Her face is flushed pink from the churning. I always dread when Mama gets out the old butter churn because the task of churning cream into butter will make your arms ache for days.

"Well hello, you two," she calls from the porch. The absence of Max is impossible to miss.

"Let me take over," Daniel offers.

"Gladly," she says. She wipes beads of sweat from her forehead and stands to hug me. It is a shame that Aunt Sadie never had children because she is a natural at it.

"How are you, honey?" she asks. She spreads her fingers across my belly, as if saying hello to the baby, too.

I tell her I'm fine but she looks over like she doesn't believe me.

"Let me make you some tea," she says. "And a big glass for you, too, Daniel?"

"Yes, please," he says. "Then I need to get back or Jo will come looking for me."

Sadie goes inside, the screen door slamming at her heels. A screen door slamming always irritates Mama, but it doesn't bother Sadie one bit. When she returns we drink tea and talk on the porch until Daniel finishes churning. He wipes his face, finishes his tea in one gulp and gets up to leave.

"I'll let your mama know where you are," Daniel says.

"Not that she cares," I say.

"Talk to her," Daniel says to Sadie.

Aunt Sadie agrees. We finish our tea and Sadie says to me, "Let's take a walk."

We walk past her garden. "The strawberries will be up in a few months," she says. "Right around the time you're due."

"I love your strawberries," I say.

"I love it when you help me pick," she replies.

"I don't know what kind of shape I'll be in this year," I say, patting my belly.

"Having a baby is not an illness," Sadie says. "It's perfectly natural. Women have been doing it for centuries."

I grow quiet, knowing that I will be a mother at thirteen and not through any choice of my own. Something about that doesn't feel so natural.

"Everything is going to work out," Sadie says. She takes my hand as we walk. "And don't you worry; your mama will come around."

"That's what Daniel says."

"Well, Daniel's right." She leans over to look at the young strawberry plants. "I've known Nell for a long time," she continues, "and she can be stubborn, that's for sure. But she's also fiercely loyal and her loyalty will win out in the end. She just needs to work through her demons, honey, and then she'll be over it. Underneath all that gruffness, your mother has a heart of gold. Joseph recognized that. That's why he married her. So don't lose faith in her. Not yet."

Even though Jesus talked about moving mountains with faith only the size of a mustard seed, I just don't have it where Mama is concerned. But I latch on to Sadie's hope and decide to leave room for a miracle, even though I don't much believe in anything anymore.

CHAPTER NINETEEN

I am almost as ripe as one of Aunt Sadie's strawberries when it comes time to pick them. The first harvest comes early this year because of an unusually hot spring. Jo is past due. We expect news any minute that the baby is coming. Despite Jo's discomfort she remains patient. Meanwhile, I do enough moaning and complaining for both of us. The last month has gone on forever and the baby is kicking up a storm. Fears torture me in the middle of the night—especially that my daughter will be more like Johnny than me and will stand down on the road, spitting into peach cans.

Sadie isn't young anymore but she can handle a whole farm on her own. She manages to get things done that would stretch two people to their limits. Selling her mountain remedies, her blackberry wine and her quilts brings money in. Her house and land she owns outright. My grandfather McAllister left Daddy and Aunt Sadie a little bit of money for land when he died. She has a hundred acres past the field and down the hillside, too steep to plow or put a house on, but it is her drug store, where she collects her ginseng root and herbs.

I crawl on my knees through the rows of strawberry plants; my belly hanging like an upside-down camel's hump. The rich, sweet earth feels solid underneath me. It is good at growing things and, for now, it looks like I am, too. I pat what I imagine to be the baby's head.

Sadie and I travel down row after row picking the fruit. I fill an old peach basket. Later we'll empty them into the kitchen sink and wash the strawberries before dividing them up and giving them to family. I grow tired quickly these days and stop to rest.

"Strawberries like the heat," Sadie says, as she wipes her face and neck with a red handkerchief. "It gets them excited about blooming."

"Then they must be absolutely thrilled," I say grumpily.

It is unbearably hot. Sweat cuts a pathway down my neck, between the cleavage I've suddenly begun to have, and over my skin stretched tight.

Sadie shoves the red handkerchief into her back pocket. As she makes her way down the rows it sways back and forth like a matador signaling a bull.

The sticky sweetness of the plants covers my hands. Every few feet Sadie scoots forward the empty flour sacks she's sewn together to use as a cushion for her knees. I have a pair, too, that look like giant potholders. Without protection, picking strawberries tears up your knees quicker than anything. The hard clay presses into hairline cuts and scrapes that turns your knees reddish orange and won't come out for days.

Sadie is in a talking mood today. From one row over, I hear about the art of canning okra and the subtle uses of ginger. She also talks about Eleanor Roosevelt, who she simply calls "Eleanor," as if they are best friends. I tune Aunt Sadie in and out like a distant radio station because I have other things on my mind. Becoming a mother worries me day and night. What if I don't know what to do?

The silence between Mama and me has become as thick as a strong strain of kudzu vine. Kudzu can take over an entire mountain in a summer. It can even swallow up an entire house if left alone. My thoughts eat away at that vine like a goat.

Sadie senses my uneasiness and sits on the ground between the rows. "I think we need a reward for all this hard work," she says.

I sit, too, wondering how I'll ever get up again.

"How about a swim?" she says.

"I'm a whale already," I say. "I'll scare the fish. Besides, I don't have a swimsuit."

"Who needs swimsuits?" she replies.

Sadie's property has private access to the lake.

"Come on," she says, offering me a hand up. My weight nearly pulls us both over and we laugh until we get upright again. Then we take our peach baskets full of strawberries and walk back to the house. On the porch we strip down to what Sadie calls *our birthday suits*. Sadie finds two towels and wraps them around us. My towel barely reaches across my belly, but nobody is around and Sadie could care less.

"Last one in is a big fat toad," she yells. Her skin, as wrinkled as mine is stretched tight, jiggles as she runs down the road, her hand clutching her towel to her chest.

The sun is straight overhead, the temperature stifling hot. The breeze that blows feels more like a heater in my face. But the river waits about a hundred yards away. Sadie is already halfway there. Her bare, white bottom shines as she runs, as if tossing a greeting in my direction.

"No fair, you got a head start," I yell. I follow her like a waddling duck, with the help of one hand braced underneath my stretched belly. When I reach the lake she is already swimming. I wade in slowly, a cautious convert.

I lower my shoulders into the river and then my head. The water baptizes me with coolness, dissolving away the sticky strawberry hotness. The bulge in my belly makes it easy for me to float. The water holds up the baby for a change instead of me. After a few minutes the tiredness leaves me and I feel light again. At this moment, I can almost remember what life was like before Johnny Monroe.

Sadie dives deep into the water, her gray braid plastered down her back. When she comes up to the surface, she is smiling.

"Your mama and I used to do this before you girls were born," Sadie says to me.

"Mama?" I ask. "It's hard to imagine her doing something so playful."

"Your mama's always been serious, even when she was young," she says. "But your daddy had a way of bringing out her carefree side. I've been worried about her since Joseph died."

"Me, too," I say. "It's like her sadness is locked deep inside and she covers it up with all the work she does to keep the family going."

Sadie takes a sideways glance at me. "When did you get to be so wise?" she asks.

Her question makes me smile and gives me a hint of hope that the secret sense may return, since it is supposed to hold wisdom.

After a while, Sadie swims to the shore and gets out of the water. She dries herself off with the towel and I get a glimpse of what it will be like looking in the mirror when I get old.

When Sadie helps me out of the water, I nearly pull her in for her efforts. But as I'm drying off, Sadie says, "The human body is amazing, isn't it? It can grow little people inside." She pats my stomach, a wide smile on her face.

I try to catch her enthusiasm but it slips like a minnow through my fingers.

After I dry off we walk back to the house hand in hand and get dressed again. While Sadie washes the strawberries in the sink, I makes us both some sweet tea. The baby moves and I stop and caress my belly.

"Is she kicking?" she asks.

"Like she's playing a drum," I say.

We both call the baby "she" after I told her about June Sector's prediction.

"It won't be long now," Sadie says. "Maybe another two or three weeks."

"Jo's due any minute," I says. "Daniel's so excited about it."

"Bringing a child into this world is a very exciting thing," she says.

"Not always," I say. I remember all the judging looks I get from the people at church, which is almost as bad as the looks of pity.

"It's a miracle no matter how she gets here," Sadie says. "And don't you for one second think otherwise."

"That sounds like what June Sector said."

"I've always liked June," Sadie says.

We stand side by side washing strawberries at the sink. I love Sadie, but deep down there is a part of me that wishes it was Mama saying and doing these things with me.

"June said this baby will grow up to be a prophet just like me," I say.

"Ooh, I like that," Sadie says, pulling the green tops off the berries.

"What do you think she meant by being a prophet?" I ask.

"That's just another name for the secret sense," Sadie says. "Someone with the secret sense just knows things a little bit before everybody else."

"You know, I haven't felt it since that day," I say.

"Just be patient, sweetheart. It will come back around, just like your mama will."

"I hope you're right," I say. Then Sadie gives me a look that is full of knowing.

"When it's time, you have someone come get me," Sadie says. "I helped your mama with all you girls."

"I'm counting on you being there," I say.

"If I remember right, you came out squalling. You had the healthiest set of lungs I've ever heard."

"Was Mama happy?" I ask.

Sadie pauses. "Yes, I'm certain she was. I seem to recall a smile on her face."

I wonder if Aunt Sadie is making this up.

"Your baby will probably come out squalling, too," she continues. "But I'll do the same with her that I did with you. I'll hold her in my arms and tell her that this world is a fine place to be and that it will hold many lessons, so she might as well quit her crying and enjoy the stay."

We wipe our hands on the same towel. "No matter what happens, Aunt Sadie, don't let Doc Lester get anywhere near me, okay?"

No love is lost between Sadie and Doc Lester. He will tell anyone who will listen that she's a "quack," because her mountain remedies eat into his profits.

"I promise," she says. "Just remember giving birth is one of the most natural things in the world. Think of those kittens being born under your porch all the time. Sometimes the mothers are no more than kittens themselves. But they know what to do when the time comes. Instinct takes over. And Louisa May *Wildflower* McAllister, you have plenty of instinct."

I lean my head into her shoulder. "Thanks, Aunt Sadie."

"You're welcome, honey."

"I guess I'd better get home," I say. "Mama's making fried chicken tonight."

"That would be enough to get me home," Aunt Sadie says. "And remember, don't let Nell get to you. She'll come around."

Before I leave Sadie picks out the best strawberries to send to Mama. It is still daylight as I walk toward home. When I pass the corner where Johnny always stood, it seems like everything that has happened in the last year has been a dream. I've moved past being so angry I could have killed Johnny myself. But I haven't stopped being angry with God, yet. Preacher is fond of saying that the road to hell is paved with regrets. I refuse to regret having this baby and I will raise her with Mama's help or without it.

CHAPTER TWENTY

A frantic knocking wakes us in the middle of the night. My breathing goes shallow. I bolt upright in bed and wait like a deer getting wind of a hunter. Unexpected noises always make me think of Johnny. Meg stashes the book under the bed she's fallen asleep with. Mama goes to the door and I hear Daniel's voice.

"It's time!" Daniel pants, as if he ran all the way up the hill.

Meg jumps up and I waddle after her.

"Has somebody gone for Sadie?" I ask.

"Nathan's on his way," Daniel says, "and Amy's meeting us at the house."

Meg and I go back to our room and dress as fast as we can. When we return to the porch, Mama has the lantern going and we follow her down the hill and across the road to Jo and Daniel's house. Every light is on inside and the whole house looks wide awake for the event. We go in the kitchen door and Mama gets busy. She gathers towels and puts water on the stove to boil while Meg and I go to the bedroom to check on Jo. Amy is already there.

Jo's face is flushed and she is sweating like it is a hundred degrees, which it might very well be. Every window is up and the curtains are open wide so more air can come in. Jo grimaces and moans with the latest labor pain, and I reach over and hold her hand. She squeezes it so hard I almost scream myself. I never realized she was so strong. Fear takes hold of me when I realize I'll be doing this same thing soon. I hold on till her pain passes then put Jo's hand in Meg's. Dizzy, I run outside, taking in big gulps of fresh air to keep from passing out.

Jo wails from inside the house as if her insides are being ripped apart. With each wail, my panic rises. I want to run and hide where nobody can find me, not even my baby that seems intent on being born, just like Jo's. I grab a lantern from the kitchen and make my way to Daniel and Jo's barn.

When I open the door, the smell of mellowed wood, dirt, and warm straw comes at me from all directions. In an odd way it reminds me of Daddy's pipe tobacco. The lantern beams out a halo of light. No animals stay in the barn anymore. Yet leather harnesses hang on rusty nails above empty feeding troths like old ghosts. Stalls empty of hay are in one corner. Daniel bought these things from the Tanners, who owned the property before them. Daniel has been saving to get a cow and maybe a goat or two, but having a baby has put that off for the time being.

It is quiet in the old barn and a little cooler. I sink to my knees near the empty horse troth in the center. If I still believed in prayer I would ask God to help me, but since he didn't help me with Johnny, I doubt he would show up for this.

Thoughts rush at me like rain pebbles blowing sideways. *I am too young to have a baby. I don't know how to do this. I don't even know how to be*

*an aunt, much less a mother to some little squalling baby that shouldn't be here
in the first place.*

Guilt and shame crash over me in a wave of fresh tears.

"Louisa May?"

I don't hear Mama come into the barn and suck in my breath
with surprise. She stands in the doorway, her lantern shining a
swatch of light right toward me. For a second, she reminds me of
the gold Mary. Then a tingle begins in my chest and it's as if the
secret sense is announcing that something big is coming. Something,
that as an old woman, I might think back on when I'm dying. I'm
not sure if it's good or bad.

"Is Jo all right?" My voice sounds small again, like it does whenever I've had the wits scared out of me.

"She still has a few more hours," she says. "But Sadie's here."

"Good," I say. Everything seems more manageable whenever
Sadie's around.

"What are you doing out here?" Mama asks. She stands a foot
away from the door, as if she can't decide whether to come in or not.

I don't feel like lying to her. The truth is, the only time I felt
worse was when Johnny beat the living daylights out of me. Except
maybe this is worse, because I am beating the living daylights out of
myself.

"Louisa May, are you all right?"

"Not really," I say.

She hesitates and then steps farther into the barn. I lower my
head to shield my eyes from the light. She can see me all too clearly
with the help of her lantern. It threatens to illuminate how scared I
am.

I wipe snot on the underside of my dress, stretched taut by the fullness of my belly. No matter how hard I try, the tears won't stop. I keep expecting her to say something about how worthless crying is, but she just stands there.

"Stop looking at me," I say. I lean into my belly and start to rock back and forth, searching for even an ounce of comfort.

She lowers the flame of the lantern, as if to offer me privacy, and walks over to me. The light and shadows make us look like giants against the back of the barn. I hate crying in front of her. I don't want to give her the pleasure of seeing me suffer.

Mama pulls an apple crate next to me and sits, and I have to resist pushing her away. I am tired of thinking of all the ways I've let her down. Not to mention all the ways she's let me down, too.

"Mama, I never should have gone out that day. I should have stayed at home. But it was Daddy's anniversary and I wanted to talk to him because I missed him so much."

I bury my head in my hands. The tears flow. I want her to touch me, to comfort me, but she doesn't. I try to convince myself that I don't care and that I'm better off without her. She is so close I can feel her breath on me.

"Louisa May, I need you to listen to me like you never have," she says. Her words are clear and strong. "Are you listening?"

"Yes, Mama, I'm listening," I say, my words aren't clear and strong at all, only soft.

Her voice softens to match mine. "Louisa May, I'm so sorry that it's taken me so long to tell you this."

She pauses and I wonder if she is about to disown me and throw me and my baby out of the only home I have ever known. She turns my head so that she can look into my eyes.

"Louisa May, you didn't do anything wrong. Do you hear me? You didn't do anything wrong. Johnny had meanness in him. You tried to tell me about him, after you heard something in the woods that night, but I didn't listen . . . Honey, I should have listened."

She starts crying, too. At first, it scares me. I thought she was too strong to cry, or too stubborn. I hug the baby as Mama's crying feels almost unbearable. Like her pain is my pain and my pain is hers. We both miss Daddy. We both have regrets about how life has turned out.

After a while, Mama wipes her tears and takes in a long, deep breath.

"It wasn't your fault that Johnny Monroe came after you," Mama begins again. "None of this was your fault. I'm sorry if I ever made you feel like it was. I just didn't know what to do, honey. I've never wanted to kill anybody so much in my life as Johnny Monroe. I wanted to take Joseph's shotgun and kill him myself. And as for Doc Lester, I admit I've done some stupid things in my life, but none quite as stupid as that. I guess it was my fear that drove me. I wanted to protect you from what everybody will say and what that precious little child will have to go through just by being born."

In that instant, I understand forgiveness. The kind Preacher said Jesus had for the people that pounded nails into his hands and hung him on the cross. I push myself through the darkness toward Mama's open arms. I fold into her, as if she is the golden Mary come to take me home. My head rests against her shoulder. I close my eyes, soaking in her love.

"We're going to be all right," Mama says. She kisses me on the cheek and rocks me in her arms. "We McAllisters are made of sturdy stock."

We sit in that old barn for a long time. After a while Mama takes another long, deep breath, and releases it, as if she suddenly understands forgiveness, too, and all the breaks between us have mended.

In the moments that follow, I feel the secret sense come alive in me again and I suddenly know that even though life will still be hard, everything is also going to be just fine. I tell Mama that I am going to name the baby Lily because her mother's name is Wildflower. Mama nods and tells me that Lily is a lovely name.

In my memory I hear Daddy playing his banjo in the living room singing an old country song that starts out sad but ends up all right. I can look on the best parts of life now, of having family with me and enough faith in myself that I can find my own way out of just about anything. Maybe someday, God and I will mend the breaks between us, too. Meanwhile, I will raise my daughter, Lily, the best way I know how.

Sequel

Did you enjoy *The Secret Sense of Wildflower*? Do you want to know more of the story? The sequel is now available!

Lily's Song

A novel
Sequel to *The Secret Sense of Wildflower*

A mother's secrets, a daughter's dream, and a family's loyalty are masterfully interwoven in this much anticipated sequel to Amazon #1 bestseller *The Secret Sense of Wildflower*.

"Wildflower" McAllister's daughter, Lily, now 14, struggles with her mother's reluctance to tell her who her father is. When a stranger appears on the family doorstep, drunk and evoking ghosts from the past, it threatens to break the close-knit McAllister family apart.

Meanwhile, Wildflower has a deep secret of her own. When Lily discovers it by accident, it changes everything she thought she knew about her mother. The events that follow silence the singing she dreamed of sharing with the world.

With her signature metaphors, Gabriel weaves a compelling tale that captures the resilience and strength of both mother and daughter, as secrets revealed test their strong bond and ultimately change their lives forever.

Set in 1956 southern Appalachia, *Lily's Song* stands on its own, and readers who are new to Gabriel will be drawn into the world she so skillfully depicts. As a sequel, it will captivate fans of *The Secret Sense of Wildflower* (a Kirkus Reviews Best Book of 2012), who have eagerly awaited more.

Praise for *Lily's Song*

"Susan Gabriel is the quintessential "Southern" writer, and gives you the full-on, sit-down-and-devour-it-novel that you came for. *Lily's Song* will resonate while you're reading and stay with you when you've finished. Highly recommended." – T. T. Thomas

"It's a beautiful story that will have you hooked from the very first. One that I could not put down until I finished it. It will stay with you long after you have finished. You will fall in love with Lily. She is not one to let things drop just because some don't want to talk about it. She wants answers and intends to have them...." - Ismore43

"Once again Susan Gabriel writes the kind of story that won't release you and invites you to return time and time again like an old friend. This is the mark of a true story teller. Having read the first book *The Secret Sense of Wildflower* and finding it very powerful, and thought provoking I was anxious to read *Lily's Song*. Susan Gabriel weaves her magic and trademark flowing prose. *Lily's Song* is, the continuation of Louisa May "Wildflower's" fourteen-year-old daughter Lily where dark secrets from the past crash full force into secrets in the present that ultimately impact everyone on Katy's Ridge." – Turtlegirl

"When Wildflower's story ended, I wanted more. I wanted to know the story of her growth to adulthood, how she would face the many problems a child with a child will encounter. I loved the characters. They were so fully developed and full of personality. It was not difficult at all to be transported to the beautiful Appalachian mountains and the life there. I wanted to stay. I was delighted to have the opportunity to read *Lily's Song* and go back to Katy's Ridge once again, and again the characters blossomed into real people. The story highlights the strength, and sadly the weakness, of the human spirit and in the end, the song soars with hope for the future." – Frances Garner

"I rarely find a book that keeps me from sleeping, eating and doing other important things throughout my days and nights, however, I kept coming back whenever I could sneak in a few minutes. To finally see how the characters evolved and always feeling like I was right there in the cabin on Katy's Ridge. Well done!" – Kimberly Goodwin

"Couldn't wait for *Lily's Song* (sequel to *The Secret Sense of Wildflower*) to be published. Sequels have a tendency to disappoint but not this one. As soon as I received the copy I began reading and literally could not put it down till I finished. Now I hate that I didn't slow down and savor it. This is well written and Lily's character is just as interesting as Wildflower." – J. Shown

Acknowledgments

There were many early readers of this manuscript before it became a tangible book. I want to thank in particular, Josephine Locklair, Jeanette Reid, Ann Bohan, Krista Lunsford and Al Mankoff, who gave me invaluable feedback in the early drafts, as well as Tommy Hayes, who teaches fiction writing in the Great Smokies Writing Program. Also, my agents, Deborah Warren and Mary Grey James of East/West Literary Agency, and Lisa Bojany Buccieri were supportive for many years. The last readers were Rich and Mary Schram who offered invaluable final thoughts and proofreading.

It takes a village, as they say, and I remain grateful for all the support I've received over the years from family, friends and wise teachers. I am especially grateful to Anne Alexander, who has believed in me when others might have given up faith. Lastly, I thank Wildflower McAllister for trusting me with her story. I hope I have done it justice.

P.S.

Insights, Interview & Reading Group Guide

About the author
Meet Susan Gabriel

About the book
Interview with Susan Gabriel
Reading Group Guide
Other Books by Susan Gabriel

About the Author

Susan Gabriel is an acclaimed writer who lives in the mountains of North Carolina. Her novel, *The Secret Sense of Wildflower*, earned a starred review ("for books of remarkable merit") from Kirkus Reviews and was selected as one of their Best Books of 2012.

She is also the author of *Temple Secrets, Grace, Grits and Ghosts: Southern Short Stories* and other novels. Discover more about Susan at SusanGabriel.com.

Interview with Susan Gabriel

What inspired you to write *The Secret Sense of Wildflower*?

The Secret Sense of Wildflower started with a voice, eleven years ago, at four in the morning, a voice that woke me up from a deep sleep. It was the voice of a girl who began to tell me her story: "There are two things I'm afraid of," she said. "One is dying young. The other is Johnny Monroe." A day or two before, I had visited the small cemetery located in the southern Appalachian Mountains where many of my family are buried. I spent an afternoon walking among the final resting places of my grandparents, aunts, uncles and cousins, as well as ancestors I had never known. It felt like I had accidentally brought one of them home with me, who needed her story told.

For a fiction writer, to get the voice of a character so clearly is really good news. I, however, wanted to go back to sleep. Who wouldn't, at 4 o'clock in the morning? For a time, I debated whether or not to get up. I ultimately decided that if I didn't claim this moment, the voice might find someone else to write her story.

Needless to say, I turned on the light, picked up a pen and a pad of paper and began to write the story of Louisa May "Wildflower" McAllister. It took months of listening to her and seeing the scenes of her life play out in my imagination. Then it took years of revising and revisiting the story to polish it and get it ready.

Which character do you feel was the most enjoyable to write?

I loved Wildflower and even miss her now that she and I aren't spending every day together. But I also loved writing about her sisters. All of them were named after the sisters in *Little Women*, which was her mother's favorite book. Aunt Sadie was the old wise woman of the story and was great fun to write, too. Old wise women have begun to show up in several of my books. In my novel *Circle of the Ancestors* it is Sam's wise grandmother who still practices the Cherokee ways. In *Temple Secrets* it is Old Sally, who has Gullah ancestors.

And then there's Daniel. God, I loved Daniel. Still do. The story needed a positive male character to balance it out. And he feels like the brother I never had. My characters often become like family members to me.

Is there a particular message in your book that you want readers to grasp?

I realized just recently, after I listed all the books I've written, that almost all of them were stories of courage and transformation. Like *The Secret Sense of Wildflower*, these are all stories about people that persevere in spite of difficult things happening to them—people who end up learning something from the experience, usually about themselves, that will help them in the future.

I was a psychotherapist for many years and one of the things I learned from my clients is how incredibly resilient people are. They would come to me with these very difficult stories of things that had happened to them and yet they had the courage to tell me about it and then try to make changes to make their lives better. That's heroic, in my view.

All my main characters (female and male) are on some kind of hero's journey. They're flawed, as we all are, but they're seeking better lives. I also have a thing for secrets. Every novel I've written has some kind of secret in it that is revealed before the book is over. For Wildflower, it's the "secret sense." Do I have secrets I keep myself? You bet. I think all of us do.

Do you have a specific writing style?

I am what we call in the business an intuitive writer. I don't use an outline, I just let the story take form in my imagination. With Wildflower, it was like watching a movie. I saw her walking through her life. I saw the story playing out like a film and simply wrote it down. I love it when stories come that way, and that's part of why I often use present tense. Sometimes the story surprises me along the way. Sometimes the endings surprise me. I rarely know the ending as I'm writing it. The creative process for me is an act of discovery. Of course, I still have to edit and polish it after that initial draft, but most of the story is there.

It's hard to pin me down in terms of genre. Mostly, I write literary fiction. *The Secret Sense of Wildflower* is considered southern gothic fiction.

What drew you to writing southern fiction?

I grew up in the South and except for a few years that I lived in Colorado, I've lived here all my life. For years, I swore that I would *never* write southern fiction. I had enough crazy "characters" in my gene pool to not want to spend any time there. But as they say: never say never. It was only after living in Colorado for three years that I discovered what a Southerner I actually was.

To me, the thing that makes southern fiction "southern," is not only that the characters are down to earth and sometimes bigger than life, but also that the land plays a big part in the stories. The landscape is often its own character and plays a central role.

Now I realize what a great honor it is to be considered a southern author. I am someone who is writing in the same genre as Harper Lee (who I've been compared to) and William Faulkner, Eudora Welty, Flannery O'Connor, Reynolds Price, as well as Ron Rash (who lives just over the next mountain ridge from where I live in the mountains of North Carolina), and a slew of others that I admire.

I also write contemporary fiction (that isn't southern), children's books and poetry.

Are you currently working on any new projects?

I am currently working on a book called *Temple Secrets*. It's a quirky southern gothic novel set in Savannah about the wealthy (white) Temple family and their black help. It is a comic novel, something I needed to write after I wrote Wildflower's story. This project will be completed in early 2015.

What do you find most challenging about writing?

Just about every professional writer today will tell you that they hate the marketing and self-promotion part. I'm basically a shy person who spends a lot of time by myself writing stories, so trying to find the attention of readers in a tidal wave of new titles is a challenge. I'm not one to toot my own horn, as they say. But I believe in Wildflower's story and if her story helps only one reader feel more hopeful and have more courage, then I'll shout it from the rooftops if I need to. I know the book has helped readers already, so I am committed to "shouting." We need fiction out there that will help us transform our own lives and take our own hero's journey.

By the way, something that readers can do when they love a book is to tell friends about it and even write short reviews at places like Amazon, Goodreads, Nook, iBooks, Audible, etc. They don't have to be long, literary reviews. They can simply say: "I loved this book!" and a sentence or two saying why. Reviews help other readers take a chance on an author or book they haven't heard of. Thanks, in advance, for considering this!

Is anything in your book based on real life experiences or purely all imagination?

I had a huge debate over this with a screenwriter once. She swore that none of her work was autobiographical, but my argument was that your work can't help but be autobiographical, simply in terms of what you notice as a writer. I notice sounds and smells and see things in a way that is totally unique to me. My imagination is the instrument I use to tell a story, so it can't help but be a reflection of me in some way. Length of paragraphs, turn of phrase, word choice, my choice of metaphors are all, in a way, my tiny fingerprint. That said, Wildflower's story is not my personal story.

What is the environment like where you write?

I live in the mountains of North Carolina, so everywhere I look are trees like oaks and wild dogwoods and every other kind of deciduous tree and pine in the southeastern United States. In the winter I can see seven mountain ridges from my office. In the summer, it's just a blur of green. My office has two giant windows and just off my office is a screened in porch, so lots of times I have sliding glass doors open to the outside. I am very lucky that I live in a beautiful place. It's a humble place, but the setting is one I love, which really helps since I spend a lot of time at home writing.

However, I don't need beautiful scenery to write. I also write anywhere that I can take a laptop or iPad with a keyboard: coffee shops, libraries, by a river, in a car, you name it. Barbara Kingsolver wrote her first novel in her bedroom closet! I haven't tried my closet, but I'll write anywhere.

What has been the most rewarding aspect of writing *The Secret Sense of Wildflower?*

I'm pretty accessible through my website and blog so people email me and tell me how moved they were by the book and how Wildflower's courage gave them hope in their own lives. That means a lot. If they take the time to email me, it is usually because they really liked the book and they'll tell me why. I've had people say about my novels that they couldn't put them down. That's always a really good sign. It means the story kept them engaged. That's a huge compliment to a writer.

On a professional level, Kirkus Reviews gave *The Secret Sense of Wildflower* a starred review (for "books of exceptional merit") and it was voted a Best Book of 2012. When I got the email about this honor I thought there must have been some kind of mistake. A switch-up in books or something. It still shocks me to this day. After all, I'd been writing in utter obscurity for almost two decades, so to have such a respected reviewer give out this kind of praise rocked my world and has opened a lot of doors for me.

But honestly, hearing from readers that they enjoyed the book means even more.

Reading Group Guide

1. As the novel opens, Louisa May "Wildflower" McAllister says, "There are two things I'm afraid of. One is dying young. The other is Johnny Monroe." What role does fear play in the story? Where did these fears originate?

2. Loss and grieving are key elements in this story. What role does loss play in the novel?

3. In Wildflower's ritual to get across the footbridge, she calls on a rabbit's food, her dead father and a gold medallion. What is the significance of the medallion in the book? What does the footbridge symbolize?

4. Wildflower constantly questions God, and especially Preacher and the self-righteous in the congregation. What role does God play in her coming-of-age?

5. How does Ruby Monroe (and what happens to her) impact Wildflower's life?

6. After Wildflower is attacked, why does she go back to her given name and refuse to be called "Wildflower" anymore?

7. Wildflower says: "Like a friend who goes away because you never listen to them, my secret sense seems to have left me,

too." Why did the "secret sense" go away? What is the significance of when it comes back? Are there any other words that you would use for the "secret sense"?

8. What role do secrets play in the story?

9. How does Wildflower's friendship with her friend, Mary Jane, evolve throughout the book?

10. What purpose does Aunt Sadie serve in Wildflower's life? Daniel and Jo? How do these close family bonds help Wildflower? How do they hurt? Did you have a favorite sister in the story? A least favorite?

11. In the final scene, Wildflower and her mother reconcile. What is the meaning of this scene? What is the significance of it taking place in the barn and her daughter being called "Lily"?

12. How does the setting—a rural mountain town in 1941 Tennessee—impact Wildflower's story?

13. *The Secret Sense of Wildflower* has been called "a quietly powerful story, at times harrowing, but ultimately a joy to read." (Kirkus—starred review) What makes this novel "quietly powerful"?

14. In the same review, the reviewer called Wildflower "an adolescent Scout Finch, had Scout's father died unexpectedly

and her life taken a bad turn" comparing *The Secret Sense of Wildflower* with *To Kill a Mockingbird*. How do you think these two books are similar?

15. What do you imagine happens in the next chapter of Wildflower's life?

16. On reader wrote: I've found a new heroine and her name is Wildflower! In what way is Wildflower brave? How can her story help others?

17. This novel has been said to "pack an emotional punch." How might the emotive quality of a story be of benefit to readers?

18. Is there anything you wish had happened in the story that didn't? What does the author do particularly well?

19. How is southern (gothic) fiction different from other genres, such as historical fiction and literary fiction?

20. Why do you think coming-of-age novels are such a popular sub-genre?

21. What does fiction offer to our modern world, as opposed to non-fiction?

Other Books by Susan Gabriel

Temple Secrets
A novel

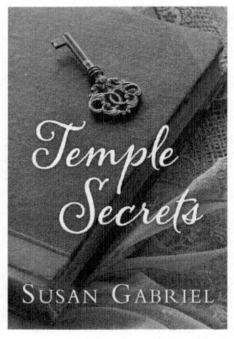

Fans of *The Help* and *Midnight in the Garden of Good and Evil* will delight in this comic novel of family secrets by acclaimed writer, Susan Gabriel.

Every family has secrets, but the elite Temple family of Savannah has more than most. To maintain their influence, they've been documenting the indiscretions of other prestigious southern families, dating as far back as the Civil War. When someone begins leaking these tantalizing tidbits to the newspaper, the entire city of Savannah, Georgia is rocking with secrets.

The current keeper of the secrets and matriarch of the Temple clan is Iris, a woman of unpredictable gastrointestinal illnesses and an extra streak of meanness that even the ghosts in the Temple mansion avoid. When Iris unexpectedly dies, the consequences are far flung and significant, not only to her family—who get in line to inherit the historic family mansion—but to Savannah itself.

At the heart of the story is Old Sally, an expert in Gullah folk magic, who some suspect cast a voodoo curse on Iris. At 100 years of age, Old Sally keeps a wise eye over the whole boisterous business of secrets and the settling of Iris's estate.

In the Temple family, nothing is as it seems, and everyone has a secret.

Now available in paperback, ebook and audiobook.

Grace, Grits and Ghosts:
Southern Short Stories

This delightful collection of short stories from acclaimed writer, Susan Gabriel (*The Secret Sense of Wildflower*, a Best Book of 2012 by Kirkus Reviews), is rich in humor, as well as mystery and meaning.

Whether white or black, living or dead, down home country or upscale urban, Gabriel's characters are quirky, poignant and deep. They include: A Gullah woman using folk magic to cast her latest spell. A girl coming-of-age dealing with death in 1940s Tennessee. A wealthy Savannah matriarch with gastrointestinal issues guarding family secrets. A good ol' boy observing himself shortly after his death. An agoraphobic woman striking up a unique friendship with the girl across the street. And a band of seventy-year-olds finding healing in a mountain stream.

Written in the tradition of Flannery O'Connor and Eudora Welty, the eight short stories in *Grace, Grits and Ghosts: Southern Short Stories* are all rooted in the southern landscape—from the steamy coast of Georgia, to the current day Atlanta suburbs, to the ancient Appalachian Mountains of North Carolina.

Pull up a rocker on the front porch, take a sip of your sweet iced tea and lose yourself in these original stories of soulful southerners and their sultry landscape.

CPSIA information can be obtained
at www.ICGtesting.com
Printed in the USA
BVOW08s1347070717
488543BV00002B/201/P